The Magic Watering Can

and

Other Stories

by

ENID BLYTON

Illustrated by
Colin Wright

AWARD PUBLICATIONS LIMITED

For further information on Enid Blyton please contact
www.blyton.com

ISBN 1-84135-062-1

This edition entitled *The Magic Watering Can and Other Stories*
published by permission of The Enid Blyton Company

This edition first published 2001
2nd impression 2002

Published by Award Publications Limited,
27 Longford Street, London NW1 3DZ

Printed in Singapore

CONTENTS

The Magic
Watering Can

Tweeky was a lazy little pixie, who yawned all day long. He always left everything till the last possible moment, and he was always putting off till the next day the things he ought to do at once.

But there was one thing he could see he really did have to do – and that was, he would certainly have to water his garden or he was going to lose all his lettuces, his peas and his carrots! The weather had been very hot and dry, and Tweeky's garden looked like a dust heap. His lettuces were drooping, his peas were turning brown, and his carrots were so tiny that they were not worth eating.

"Bother!" said Tweeky, looking at his dry garden. "I suppose I must water today – but what a nuisance it is, to be sure! How I hate carrying a heavy watering can to and fro, to and fro! If only I had a spell I could put into my can which would make it water the whole garden by itself!"

Now, no sooner had he thought that, than an idea popped into his head. Why not go to Mother Lucy and ask her for a spell? She probably wouldn't give him one – but she might. So off he went, three doors away, to ask her.

But she was out. There was no one in her little yellow cottage at all. Tweeky peeped inside the door and saw her neat kitchen, with all its shelves and drawers, each one labelled. He tiptoed inside and read the labels.

"Ha!" he said suddenly. "Just look at that label – 'A spell for watering cans and hosepipes, taps and hot-water jugs'! That's just what I want!"

He looked round. No one could see him – so the naughty little pixie opened the drawer, took out one of the small blue spells that were neatly lying in rows

there, and hurriedly shut the drawer again. He ran out and went back to his cottage.

He looked at the spell. It was like a small lump of sugar, but blue instead of white. He knew exactly what to do with it. He fetched his can, filled it half full of water, popped the blue lump of sugar into it and shook it well, saying, "Water, water, pour without stopping!"

Then he took the can to his lettuce-bed and tipped it up to water with it. He let go of the handle and the can stayed all by itself in the air, watering steadily, moving along the row of lettuces slowly as it did so. It was wonderful to see. It never seemed to get empty – there seemed to be a marvellous amount of water in it, and Tweeky knew it would never stop so long as the spell was in the can.

"Now I shall sit down in my garden-chair and have a nice lazy read," said Tweeky to himself. "That can is going to do all my work for me!"

So he sat down in his chair and began

to read his book. But the sun was hot and Tweeky began to yawn. Soon he was fast asleep.

The watering can went steadily on with its work, and a splash-splash sound was heard for a long time. The can watered the lettuces, the carrots, and the peas. Then it watered the patch of grass. Then it moved to the little gravel path and watered that so thoroughly that it soon turned into a running river!

Tweeky slept soundly. The can went inside the cottage and began to water the pot-plants there. Then there really was nothing else for it to do, so it began to water the things it shouldn't!

It watered the kitchen fire and put it out with a sizzle! It watered Tweeky's bed and made it soaking wet! It poured streams of water over his dinner-table, which was still littered with dirty dishes. Goodness, what a mess it made! Then it filled the waste-paper basket full of water, and drenched all the cushions on the chairs. Gracious me, that watering can had a wonderful time, I can tell you!

Now after some time Tweeky woke up and remembered the can. He looked round to see where it was. He saw the soaked gravel path, which still looked like a stream, and he felt cross.

Wherever was that can?

Then he heard a noise of splashing inside his cottage and he jumped up in a flash. Surely that wicked watering can hadn't dared to go inside his cottage!

He rushed indoors – and oh, what a

sight he saw! Everything was running with water, his fire was out, and the can was just watering Tweeky's nice new suit!

Tweeky rushed at the can, and it turned on him and watered him from head to foot! He caught hold of the handle and pulled the can to him. He put his hand into the water to get out the spell – but dear me, it had melted just like sugar! Tweeky groaned. He

knew there was only one thing to do now
– he must go and confess to Mother Lucy
and ask her to stop the spell somehow!

He carried the can to Mother Lucy's
and it poured water on his feet all the
way. She was in, and she was most
surprised to hear the tale that Tweeky
sobbed out to her.

"Everything's spoilt – my new suit,
my cushions; my fire's out, my whole
house is running with water! I fell asleep,

you see. Oh, Mother Lucy, I know it was very wrong to borrow that spell when you were out, but please do forgive me and help me, for I have been well punished!"

Mother Lucy blew into the can and whispered a magic word. A piece of blue sugar slowly began to appear at the bottom of the water. She slipped in her hand and took it out. At once the can stopped watering and stayed quite still.

"I won't punish you any more," said Mother Lucy, who had a kind heart. "I am sure you are punished enough already by having a house that is soaking wet everywhere. You will have a busy time clearing out everything, Tweeky, and drying it. My, won't you have to work hard for a long time! Well, it won't hurt you, for you have always been a lazy fellow. Perhaps this will teach you to be better in future!"

"Oh, it will, it will!" said poor Tweeky. And it certainly did! Tweeky isn't lazy any more, and he works hard every day. He has never borrowed anything again without asking, either. As for his watering can, he gave it away and bought a new one. He simply couldn't bear to see the old one sitting on the shelf, grinning at him!

Mr Twiddle and
His Wife's Hat

One day Mrs Twiddle wanted to take her hat back to the hat-shop because she didn't like the red roses on it.

"I would much rather have violets on my new hat," she said to Mr Twiddle. "Don't you think violets would be nicer than roses, Twiddle?"

"Well, dear, hollyhocks and sunflowers are very beautiful too," said Mr Twiddle, looking out into his garden proudly, where his hollyhocks were flowering very tall and straight, and his giant sunflowers were growing as high as the house, though they were not yet out.

"Twiddle! Do you think I would put hollyhocks and sunflowers on a hat?" cried Mrs Twiddle. "Do, for goodness sake, think what you are saying!"

"I *was* thinking," said Mr Twiddle, offended. "And I think that sunflowers and hollyhocks are—"

"All right, all right!" said Mrs Twiddle quickly, because she didn't want to hear it all again. She picked up her new hat with red roses.

"You don't think it would be nice to have feathers on my hat instead of flowers, do you?" she asked.

"No, I don't," said Mr Twiddle, who was very fond of birds and hated to see their feathers in people's hats. "Why don't you have mouse-tails or something like that? I wouldn't mind seeing mouse-tails in your hat at all."

"Twiddle, don't be horrid," said Mrs Twiddle. "You know how afraid of mice I am. I should run miles if I had their tails on my head."

Mr Twiddle thought it would be fun to see fat little Mrs Twiddle run miles. He began to think how he could get some mouse-tails for her. But Mrs Twiddle didn't give him any time to think.

"I shall go back to the shop now," she said. "You come with me, Twiddle, there's a dear, and you shall help me to choose new flowers for my hat. You can carry the hatbox for me, too. That will be a great help."

"Very well," said Mr Twiddle. He watched Mrs Twiddle put her hat carefully into a box full of white tissue paper.

"You tie the box up for me, Twiddle, while I go and get ready," said Mrs Twiddle. Off she ran, and Mr Twiddle looked round for some string. There was none in the string-box, of course. There never was. Mr Twiddle thought he had some in the woodshed outside, so out he went.

Now when the kitchen was empty, Mrs Twiddle's big black cat walked in. He simply loved playing with paper of any sort, so when he saw the white tissue paper sticking out of the hatbox he ran over to it at once. He pulled at it and the lid fell off. That made him jump. He crouched back, and then sprang at the box. He landed right inside it, on top of the hat.

"Mee-ow-ee-ow!" said the cat, pleased. It began to play with one of the red roses. It burrowed right underneath the white paper. It had a simply lovely time!

Mr Twiddle was a long time finding the string. The cat played with the roses till it was tired. Then it settled down inside the hat, with all the tissue paper on top of it. It tucked its nose into itself and went to sleep. It loved sleeping on paper.

Presently Mrs Twiddle bustled into the room, all ready to go out. She called

Mr Twiddle. "Twiddle, Twiddle! What in the world are you doing? I'm just going to get my coat."

Mr Twiddle came running in with a long piece of string. "I've been hunting for string," he said. "Really, this is a dreadful house for string. Never a bit to be found!"

"Well, hurry and tie up the hatbox," Mrs Twiddle said impatiently. "You always take such a time over doing everything!"

Mr Twiddle put the lid on the box quickly. He tied it up firmly. He picked up the box, and set off after Mrs Twiddle, who was already walking down the garden path.

The box felt very heavy. Surprisingly heavy, Mr Twiddle thought. He simply couldn't understand it. How brave women were to wear such heavy hats on their heads! He began to puff and pant.

"Twiddle! What are you puffing like that for?" Mrs Twiddle cried in surprise. "It's not such a hot day as all that, surely!"

"Your hat is so heavy," said poor Mr Twiddle, who didn't know he was carrying a very large cat as well as the hat.

"Twiddle! How can you say that my little straw hat is heavy!" said Mrs Twiddle. "What a fuss you do make! I'm ashamed of you."

Mr Twiddle went redder than he already was. He hated Mrs Twiddle to be ashamed of him. He took the box in both arms and panted along.

But really, it was frightfully heavy.

"I shall have to have a rest, dear," said Mr Twiddle when they came to the seat by the bus stop. "This box is so very heavy, really."

"I hate stopping here," said Mrs Twiddle. "The bus seat is just outside the fish-shop, and I don't like the smell."

But Mr Twiddle meant to have a rest, so he sat down, putting the box on his knee to leave room for other people on the seat. Mrs Twiddle sat down too. She turned up her nose at the smell of the fish in the fish-shop.

The cat woke up when it smelled the fish. It was very fond of fish. It thought it would be nice to taste some, so it began to wriggle round the box to find a way to get out.

Mr Twiddle was rather alarmed. The box seemed to be coming alive! It moved on his knee. It shook and wriggled. Mr Twiddle held it tightly, for he really thought it was going to jump off his knee.

"What's the matter now, Twiddle?" said Mrs Twiddle, noticing that Mr Twiddle looked frightened.

"Well, my dear, your hat is not only very heavy but it seems to be walking round the box," said poor Mr Twiddle.

"Walking round the box!" cried Mrs Twiddle. "Whatever will you say next? You know perfectly well that a hat can't walk round a box."

"It seems to be jumping up and down in the box now," said Mr Twiddle, beginning to tremble. The cat was doing its very best to get out. It mewed quietly a few times.

"The hat is talking," said Mr Twiddle. "I'm glad it's not my hat. I wouldn't wear a heavy, talking, walking, jumping hat like this for anything!"

The cat suddenly went quite mad and began to leap round and round the box, scratching at the paper as it went. Mr Twiddle couldn't bear it any longer. He threw the box into the road!

Mrs Twiddle jumped up with a scream. "Oh, my new hat, my new hat!" she cried, and she ran to get it. She picked up the box and took it back to the seat. It did feel very heavy. It did feel as if the hat was leaping about. How very extraordinary! Mrs Twiddle undid the string with trembling fingers and took off the lid.

Out leaped the big black cat with a howl, scratched Mrs Twiddle on the hand, and flew off down the road with its tail straight up in the air!

"Was that a cat or my hat?" wept poor Mrs Twiddle, putting a hanky round her hand.

"It was your cat," said Mr Twiddle, glaring after the running animal. "That cat! It's always getting into mischief.

Now perhaps you will say you're sorry to
me, for making me carry your cat such a
very long way!"

"Well, perhaps you'll say you're sorry
to me for putting a cat into my hatbox,
and letting it sit on my new hat!" sobbed
Mrs Twiddle, taking a very squashed hat
out of the box. "It's chewed the roses!"

"I shan't say I'm sorry, but I'll buy you some new violets for the hat," said kind Mr Twiddle, who was upset to see his wife so unhappy. "Come along."

"Well, I shan't say I'm sorry then, but I'll buy you a kipper for your tea," said Mrs Twiddle, wiping her eyes.

So Mrs Twiddle had her violets and Mr Twiddle got his kipper – but, as I dare say you will guess, the big black cat got nothing at all except a good slap when he came in to sniff at the kipper!

Jimmy's Robin

In Jimmy's garden lived a fine cock robin. You should have seen him! He had a beautiful red breast and the brightest black eyes, and he flew down beside Jimmy every time the little boy went to dig in his garden.

Jimmy gave the robin crumbs each day, and he often sang a little sweet song to Jimmy, and once, for just a moment, he flew on to Jimmy's head and stood there! Wasn't that friendly!

Then one day Jimmy was ill. He had to go to bed, and the little robin missed him badly. He hunted all over the garden for Jimmy, but he was nowhere to be seen. So the robin thought he would go and look in the house. Perhaps Jimmy was there!

He looked in all the windows – and at last he found Jimmy, lying in bed, looking very miserable, for the little boy was lonely. The robin flew in at the open window and then sat on the bottom of Jimmy's bed.

"Tweet, tweet, chirry, chirry, chee!" he sang. Jimmy opened his eyes and sat up in delight.

"Why, it's my robin!" he said. "Oh, robin, how nice of you to come and find me! It's been so dull lying here in bed! Do come and see me every day!"

"Tweet, tweet, I will!" said the robin.

He flew down on to Jimmy's blanket and sang a little song there and then he flew out of the window again. He had thought of such a good idea! He had a little wife and they were looking for a good place to build their nest. What fun it would be if they could find a place in Jimmy's bedroom! Jimmy was such a nice boy, and the little robin would like to build somewhere near his friend.

He found his wife and told her his good idea. Then together they flew back to Jimmy's bedroom and looked into every nook and corner to see if they could find a good place to put their nest.

"What about behind this bookcase by Jimmy's bed?" said the robin. "There is just room."

"Tweet, chirry chee!" said his wife. "Yes, that will be fine!"

So, for the next few days, Jimmy had a lovely time, watching the little robins build their nest in his bedroom! He didn't tell anyone, because he was afraid that his mother might say they were making a mess. He just lay and watched the little birds fly in and out – sometimes with a wisp of root, sometimes with two or three dead leaves, sometimes with a bit of moss.

One day the robin pecked a few hairs out of Jimmy's hairbrush! Jimmy did laugh! The hairs went into the nest too. Then the robin's wife sat down on her cosy nest behind the bookcase and laid four pretty, red-spotted eggs. Jimmy could just see them if he peeped behind the bookcase. It really was very exciting!

"I can't understand how it is that Jimmy is so good and happy, staying all this time in bed!" said his mother to the doctor. "He is just as good as gold!"

Jimmy knew why he was so happy and good. It was because he had two friends living behind his bookcase. But he wasn't going to say a word!

One day the eggs hatched out into tiny baby birds. The two robins sang loudly for joy. Jimmy sang for joy too! He was just as pleased as the robins. He peeped behind the bookcase and looked at the baby birds each day. Sometimes the two robins would fly off to get food for them, and Jimmy would look after them. He promised the robin that he would not let Pussy come into the room.

And then the little robins grew so big that it was time for them to fly away. And do you know, they all got out of the nest and flew about the room! Just imagine that! Jimmy laughed so loudly – and just at that moment his door opened and in came Mother with the doctor!

"Well!" said Mother, in surprise.

"Wherever did all these birds come from?"

And then Jimmy had to tell his mother about the nest and show her and the doctor where it was built behind the bookcase. Mother was so surprised!

"But I am very sad now," said Jimmy, "because, you see, the babies are flying away and I won't see the robins any more. They will be about the garden, with their father and mother. It is time they flew out of this room."

"And it is time you flew out of this room too!" said the doctor, smiling. "It is lovely sunny weather and you are to lie out in the garden all day long now – so you will be able to see your robins all the time!"

Jimmy was so pleased – and now he and the robins are in the garden together, and Jimmy is nearly well again. He has six tame robins – isn't he lucky?

The
Disobedient Doll

The silly sailor doll never did as he was told. He was the silliest, most disobedient toy in the playroom. He just didn't care for anybody!

The big teddy bear was head of the playroom, and all the toys except the sailor doll took notice of what he said, and were careful to obey him. But the sailor doll only laughed at him!

"Never, ever, play with matches," said the teddy bear. "They are very, very dangerous." So nobody did – except the silly sailor doll! He found a matchbox and struck every single match in it. He even set fire to a piece of jigsaw and burned it all up. It was lucky nothing else caught fire.

The bear was very angry. "Now the

children won't be able to finish the picture which that bit of jigsaw belongs to," said the bear. "You are very naughty, Sailor Doll, and very, very silly."

Another time the bear saw that some fireworks in a box had been put into the toy-cupboard, ready for a party.

"You must never play with these," he said. "They could go off, and you would hurt yourself or someone else very badly!"

Well, of course, you can guess that the silly sailor doll at once got the box, opened it, and took out a firework. There were no more matches to light it with and so he threw it at the wall. It went bang, threw out some silver sparks all over the red-haired doll, burned her hair, and then landed on the teddy bear. The sailor doll laughed till he cried at the poor burnt doll, which really was horrible of him.

The bear chased him all round the playroom, but he couldn't catch the bad sailor doll because he climbed up on to the windowsill. The big teddy bear was

too fat to climb all the way up there.

"You wait!" he said to the sailor doll. "One of these days you'll get a shock, Sailor Doll, and you'll deserve to!"

"And one of these days you'll get a hundred," said the silly sailor doll, laughing. "You got a fine one tonight, didn't you, Teddy?"

"Don't take any notice of him," said the rabbit. "All he wants is to be noticed. Leave him alone and then maybe he will decide to become better."

Well, it was quite true – the silly sailor doll hated not to be looked at and spoken to. He was very vain and he loved to shock people. He tried all he could to make the toys notice him, but they just turned their heads away and wouldn't look at him at all.

Then a new toy came to the playroom. It was a blue aeroplane. It belonged to Billy. The sailor doll was very interested in it, for he thought it must be wonderful to fly in the air like a bird.

The aeroplane flew swiftly round the playroom and Billy was very pleased with it. He showed it to his sister, Shirley. "Look," he said, "if you want to make it fly, you wind this long elastic round and round and round underneath the

aeroplane. Then you hold it up like this – let it go – and the elastic unwinds quickly and sends the plane flying through the air. Isn't it clever?"

All the toys thought the aeroplane was marvellous, especially the sailor doll. That night they all stood round the blue plane and looked at it.

"It would be quite easy to fly it," said the rabbit. "Just wind up the elastic and off it goes."

"Nobody is to fly this aeroplane," said the teddy bear at once. "We might break it. It looked easy when we saw Billy doing it, but it might not be so easy if we tried."

"Very well, Teddy," said the toys. "We won't fly it."

Only the sailor doll didn't promise. He just longed and longed to fly the aeroplane – and what was more, he longed to go with it!

So whatever do you think he did? He went to the doll's swing in the corner and took away the little seat with ropes! The rabbit saw him and told the teddy bear.

"Oh, don't take any notice of him," said the bear crossly. "He just wants some attention. He can't get into any mischief with the swing."

But the sailor doll could! He tied the ropes of the swing seat to the underneath of the aeroplane. That was to be his seat, you see, when the aeroplane flew off. It would take the swing seat with it, and the sailor doll thought he would have a wonderful time flying round the playroom.

Then the sailor doll wound up the elastic, pulling very tightly indeed. None of the toys looked to see what he was doing. They obeyed the bear and took no notice of him at all.

Whirrrr-rrr-rrr-rrr! The aeroplane flew off into the air. *Whir-rrr-rrr!* It flew all round the playroom, and the sailor doll flew too, sitting in the little toy swing seat below. My word, what excitement! *Whirr-rrr-rrr!* The aeroplane flew right out of the window and into the blackness of the night!

"I say! We'll have to take a bit of notice

now!" cried the rabbit. "The aeroplane has gone out of the window, and that monkey of a sailor doll has gone with it!"

Crash! A loud noise came in at the window, and the toys went pale and looked at one another in fright. The aeroplane had crashed!

"I suppose we shall just have to go and look for it," said the teddy bear. So they helped Teddy up on to the windowsill and they all climbed out of the window and hurried to find the aeroplane. The teddy bear was clever enough to take Billy's little torch with him, and he switched it on and looked all round.

"There's the aeroplane – look!" cried the rabbit. And sure enough, there it was on the ground, upside down. But there was no sign of the sailor doll anywhere.

The toys looked at the plane. It didn't seem to be hurt at all. It had bumped into a holly bush and had fallen to the ground. The toys thought they could get it back into the playroom all right. But they couldn't untie the knots

40

that tied the swing seat to the aeroplane. So they had to leave them but they couldn't help wondering what Billy and Shirley would say the next day, when they saw it!

Then they heard somebody crying, and the bear flashed his torch about to find the sailor doll. Where do you think he was? Up in the prickly holly bush, hanging by his trousers! He had fallen out when the aeroplane had flown into the tree and the prickles were holding him tightly.

"Help me! Help me!" wept the sailor doll. "Get me down! The holly is pricking me dreadfully!"

"We can't possibly get you down," said the bear. "Who do you suppose is going to climb a prickly holly bush to rescue a bad doll like you? You'll have to stay there. I'm sorry, but we just can't help it!"

They all went back to the playroom, carrying the aeroplane. They managed to

get it in at the window. The sailor doll was left outside.

It began to rain and he got wet. The rain trickled down his neck. The holly pricked him. He felt very cold and damp. He was frightened, because a spider ran over him and asked if she could spin her web from his nose right down to his toes!

"Why have I been so bad? Why did I disobey the bear?" he sobbed. "This really is dreadful! A-tish-oo! Now I'm getting a horrible cold! Oh, if only I could get back into the nice, warm playroom, I would never, ever be disobedient again!"

The rain stopped. The wind began to blow. How it blew! The holly bush shook from top to bottom. It stuck its prickles into the doll harder than ever.

The wind blew so hard that the doll was afraid of falling. He tried to take hold of the holly leaves to stop himself from falling, but they were so prickly that he had to let go. And down he went to the ground! The prickles tore his clothes as he went. The ground bumped him hard. At last he picked himself up,

and sneezing and snuffling he limped back to the playroom. He climbed in at the window.

"Ah! Here's the bold adventurer back again!" said the teddy bear. "I hope you enjoyed yourself, Sailor Doll."

"Well, I didn't," sniffed the doll. "A-tish-oo! A-tish-oo! I'm wet. I'm cold. I'm torn. I'm prickled. Whatever shall I do?"

"Get into the doll's cot and keep warm then," said the rabbit, who had a kind heart. "You do look dreadful, Sailor Doll! I shouldn't be at all surprised if you get thrown into the dustbin tomorrow!"

"Ohhh!" squealed the sailor doll in fright. He crept into the doll's cot and drew the bedclothes round him. He soon fell asleep, though he even sneezed in his sleep!

Next day Billy and Shirley found the swing seat tied under the aeroplane and they guessed one of the toys had been for a flight. When they found the wet, torn sailor doll, they knew at once that it was he who had taken the aeroplane for a flight.

Shirley gave him a good telling off. "You might have broken the aeroplane," she said. "Teddy! You are the head of the playroom. Just see that it doesn't happen again!"

But he doesn't need to bother, for the sailor doll has had such a fright that he says he'll never be naughty or silly again. He will never play with matches or fireworks or anything like that and he still can't help sneezing every time he thinks of that horrible, cold, wet night!

The Hole in
the Mackintosh

Jack and Mollie were very excited. It was their mother's birthday the next day and they were going to buy her a little brooch they had seen in a shop window. It had "Mother" written on it, and they thought it was just the right thing to get.

It was five pounds and they had saved that up together in their money-box. They had saved up three pounds more besides, so they thought they would buy her a bunch of flowers, too.

"We'll go and buy the brooch and the flowers after school this afternoon," said Mollie. "We'll get a birthday card as well, and let's write out a nice card that we can tie on to the flowers, Jack."

So Mollie wrote in her best writing *With Love to Mummy on her Birthday*

across a pretty picture postcard.

"Time for school," their mother called out. They quickly emptied all their money into a little purse and put the card with it.

"I'll take it," said Mollie.

"No, let me," said Jack. "Girls lose things."

"So do boys," said Mollie. "Oh, do let me take the purse and the card."

47

"No, I shall put them into the right-hand pocket of my mackintosh, with my new marbles and my bag of toffees," said Jack.

He slipped on his brown mackintosh, and put the purse with the money, and the postcard too, into his pocket. He felt the marbles and the toffees there as well. "Come on!" he said. "We shall be late for school."

They ran off. All through afternoon school they were thinking of what fun they would have buying the brooch for their mother. They were the first in the cloakroom when school was over. They dragged on their mackintoshes and rushed out.

"We shall have plenty of time to go and buy the brooch and the bunch of flowers," cried Jack.

They ran to the jeweller's shop first, and looked into the window. Yes, the brooch was still there. They went into the shop and asked for it. The jeweller took it out of the window. It really was beautiful, all made of silver.

"Please could you put it into a box and we'll take it now," said Jack, feeling most important. He put his hand into his pocket to take out the purse – and, oh my goodness me, it wasn't there! He felt wildly round and round his pocket – but all he managed to find was a great big hole!

"What's the matter?" asked Mollie. "Oh, Jack – you haven't lost the money?"

"There's nothing in my pocket at all," Jack said miserably. "Only just a hole.

You feel. Everything must have slipped through it – the purse, the card, my new marbles and my toffees. Oh, Mollie!"

"We can't have the brooch for Mummy," said Mollie, tears in her eyes. "And we saved up for such a long time, Jack. Oh, I wish you had let me take the money when I asked you."

"Well, I'm sorry, children, but I'm afraid I can't let you have the brooch if you haven't the money to pay for it," said the jeweller, and he put the brooch back into the window again.

Poor Jack and Mollie. They walked sadly home, both of them crying. It was so very disappointing – and now they had nothing for their mother's birthday at all.

Just as they reached home Mother came out to them.

"Jack!" she called. "Have you taken Billy Brown's mackintosh by mistake? He has just been here with yours, and he thinks you must have taken his, you were in such a hurry. See, your name is on the collar."

Jack and Mollie stared at their mother – and then Mollie gave a shout.

"Jack!" she cried. "Perhaps everything is in the pockets after all. Quick! Take the mackintosh from Mummy and look. You've got the wrong one on. You must have taken Billy's by mistake, and that's why there was a big hole in the pocket."

Jack took the mackintosh from Mother and slipped his hand in the right-hand pocket – and oh! What a lovely surprise! The purse, the card, his new marbles and his bag of toffees were all there. He had taken Billy's coat because he had been in such a hurry, and had left his own coat hanging on the peg.

"The two mackintoshes are exactly the same," said Mollie. "Take off the one you've got on, Jack, and have a look to see if Billy's name is on it."

Jack slipped it off straight away – and sure enough, there was Billy Brown's name on the collar.

"You silly boy," said Mother. "You had better run to Billy's with his mackintosh this very minute, or he will have to go out in the rain without it. Tea isn't quite ready yet so you've got plenty of time."

Off went the two children, as happy as could be. Jack had on his own mackintosh this time, and the purse and everything was safely in his pocket. They left the other mackintosh at Billy's and then tore off to the jeweller's again.

They bought the brooch and then went to the flower-shop and bought five

beautiful red roses. They tied the card to them, and went home. They went upstairs and hid the roses and the brooch and then went down to tea.

"What were you crying about when you came in before?" asked Mother.

"Oh! We can't tell you till tomorrow," said Jack. "It's a secret."

You should have seen how pleased Mother was the next day with her lovely brooch and roses. She hugged Mollie and Jack and thanked them very much. She said she liked the brooch and the roses best of all her presents.

"But we nearly didn't get them," said Jack, and he told his mother all about the wrong mackintosh with the hole in the pocket. "Wasn't it a good thing Billy found out my mistake?"

And Mother said it really was a very good thing indeed.

Bumble and
the Elves

Mr Bumble was having some painting
and whitewashing done in his cottage.
Mrs Bumble had said that really the walls
were getting dreadfully dirty, and the
ceilings weren't fit to be seen, so Bumble
had said he would have the house all
nicely painted, with some lovely new
wallpaper in the parlour.

"I'll get the painter elves in to do the
walls and ceilings of every room except
the parlour," he said. "I don't think they
would be much good at papering. I shall
do the papering!"

Mrs Bumble looked at Bumble, and
wrinkled her rosy face.

"Oh, Bumble," she said, "do you think
you ought to? You know you're not very
good at doing things for the house. Don't

you remember when you tried to paint the shed? You lost the paint five times, couldn't find your brush, and ended up by stepping into the paint-pot and spoiling your new shoes."

"Fiddlesticks!" said Bumble crossly. "This is a very different sort of job. I shall be most careful. All I need is some rolls of pretty wallpaper, a pot of good paste, and a paste-brush. I don't think I can get into much trouble with that, can I?"

The next week the painter elves came in to start painting the house. They were a lively lot and Bumble didn't like them very much because they were not very polite to him. They wanted to tell him the best way to paper the parlour, too, and he didn't want any help from anyone.

The very first day he started on his work he made a bad mistake. He didn't look carefully enough at the paper he was putting on the wall, and when one of the elves peeped in to see how he was getting on, how he laughed!

"Oh, Mr Bumble!" he cried. "You've

gone and put that piece on upside down!"

And so he had! He stared at it angrily and then tore it off. "I'm sure I had it the right way up when I measured it on the wall," he growled to himself. "Perhaps one of those cheeky little elves popped in and put it the wrong way up for me. I shouldn't be a bit surprised."

The next day the elves peeped in again, and found Bumble in great trouble. He could not seem to make the paper stick on the wall. It fell off as fast as he pasted it on. The elves looked at his paste-pot and then laughed heartily.

"Oh dear, oh dear, that Mr Bumble's a funny old man!" they giggled. "He's trying to paste his paper on the wall with Mrs Bumble's furniture polish!"

Bumble looked down at his pot – and to his surprise and disgust he saw that he had been using the polish-pot instead of the paste-pot! No wonder the paper wouldn't stick to the wall! The paste-pot was standing in the corner where he had put it the day before.

Bumble was very angry when he heard the elves laughing. He shook his brush at them and told them to go away.

"Back to your work!" he cried. "I believe it was one of you who played this trick on me, putting the pot of polish for me to use, instead of my paste-pot! Yes, you're a set of tiresome nuisances! Be off to your work in the next room!"

The elves went, looking rather scared. Bumble certainly had a bad temper!

Now the next day Bumble worked very hard indeed – so hard that after a little while he needed a rest. So he put his paste-brush down on a chair – which he

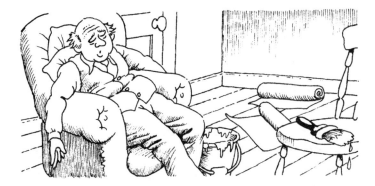

certainly shouldn't have done for it made
a mess – sat down in another chair and
closed his eyes for a little nap.

While he was gently snoring, Mrs
Bumble came in to ask him what he
would like to have for his supper that
night. When she saw Bumble was asleep,
she smiled, and sat down patiently on a
chair to wait for him to wake up. She
took out her knitting and began to knit.

Now, although she didn't know it, she
had sat down on the very sticky paste-
brush! Mrs Bumble was fat, and wore
very wide, full skirts, and she had no
idea at all that she was sitting on the
paste-brush. She sat there, knitting
quietly – and then someone came to the

back door. Up got Mrs Bumble and went to see who it was, the paste-brush sticking to her skirt. She let the parlour door bang and that woke up Bumble with a jump.

"Dear, dear!" he said, opening his eyes and yawning. "I've been to sleep. This will never do! I must get on with my work!"

He looked for his paste-brush and it wasn't there! Then how angry he was! "It's those tiresome little elves!" he cried. "They've slipped in here while I was asleep and taken my brush!"

He rushed into the next room. "Where's my brush?" he cried to the startled elves. "Come, don't look so surprised! I know you've taken it. Give it to me at once or I'll punish you!"

"We certainly haven't got your brush," said the elves, and no matter what Bumble said, they stuck to that. They had not got his brush.

"Very well," said Bumble, looking very fierce. "I shall now put a spell on whoever has it. That will teach you a lesson, you mischievous creatures!"

He waved his hands in the air. "May whoever has the brush be punished by it!" he cried. "May he be slapped in the face by it! May he be pushed on the nose by it! May he be pasted from head to foot!"

He stopped and glared at the elves, to see which one would be punished – and at that very moment there came dreadful shrieks from the kitchen, where poor Mrs Bumble was making a cake. The paste-brush had suddenly jumped up, and was slapping her on the face, and

covering her with paste! She pushed it away with her hands, but it came back again and again, till she was sticky from head to foot. She rushed into the room where Bumble and the elves stood listening in surprise to her screams, and called out to Bumble, "Look at your paste-brush! Make it stop, make it stop!"

Bumble stared in horror. Then he said a few magic words and the brush hopped peacefully into its pot where it stayed.

And then, what a bad time Bumble had, explaining to Mrs Bumble what had happened! How angry she was! How she scolded poor Bumble!

"I must have sat on your nasty brush when I came into the parlour for a few minutes," she said. "What do you want to leave a paste-brush on a chair for, you silly creature? That's the end of your paper hanging, Bumble! Go to the bedroom and tidy all your drawers and cupboards. That will keep you out of mischief. Elves, you can paper the parlour as soon as you've finished your other work!"

Poor Mr Bumble! He was glad when all the work was finished, for you have no idea how those elves chuckled and laughed whenever they saw him creeping quietly about the house! He did feel ashamed of himself!

Catch Him
Quick

"Would you like to see my pet white mice, Ian?" asked Alice, when Ian came to tea one afternoon.

"Oooh, yes," said Ian. "I'm not allowed to keep pet mice – but I wish I was. I do like them."

"I'll get mine. They're called Bubble and Squeak," said Alice. "I'll bring them up to my playroom. You wait here."

She had soon brought the two white mice in their little cage. They were so tame that they ran all over Alice and Ian, and twitched their little pink noses as they sniffed about here, there and everywhere.

"Oh, I do wish I had two lovely little mice like these," said Ian. "I really do."

After a while Mother called out that their

64

tea was ready. "We'd better put the mice back into their cage and go," said Alice. "We'll play with them again afterwards."

The two mice were quickly put back into their cage. Alice swung the little door shut and latched it. Then they went downstairs to have their tea.

But Alice hadn't latched the door properly. It swung open – and the mice were easily able to get out! Squeak didn't want to get out. She was always afraid of cats when the playroom was empty. But Bubble was much bolder. He ran out at once.

The toys had been very interested, watching the two mice while the children were playing with them. Now, when Bubble came running out, the sailor doll sat up in a hurry.

"Catch him, quick! He's escaping! The children will be very upset if they find him gone."

"Catch me if you can!" said Bubble and scampered about the playroom floor. The sailor doll chased him. The teddy bear tried to head him off. The curly-haired doll tried to trap the naughty mouse in a corner.

But the mouse was much too clever to be caught. He ran here, he ran there – he laughed at the toys, and not one of them could manage to catch him.

"There he goes. Catch him, quick!" shouted the sailor doll again, as the mouse rushed out from under the couch.

Off they all went, after the mouse. Just as they thought they had finally got him, he slipped away again.

"Can't catch me! Can't catch me!" he called.

The sailor doll stopped, out of breath. He thought hard for a minute. Then a big grin spread over his handsome face.

He whispered to the bear. "I've got an idea. I'm going to hide behind the curtain where no one will see me. And I'm going to make a noise like a cat!"

"Ooooh, Sailor Doll! That is a good idea!" said the bear. "That will give the naughty little mouse such a fright. He will go rushing back to his cage at once!"

The sailor doll slipped quietly behind the curtain. Then he began to mew.

"Meeow-ee-ow-ee-ow! Meeow! Meeow!"

The mouse stopped short at once and looked round anxiously for the cat. But he couldn't see it anywhere.

"Meeow-ee-ow!" mewed the sailor doll, trying his hardest not to laugh. The mouse gave a squeal and looked at his cage. Dare he run right across the floor to it? Would the cat catch him as he went across? Well, he must try.

He scampered across the floor – and the sailor doll mewed again. The scared mouse turned aside and ran into the doll's-house! The little front door was open, so he got in easily.

"He's in the doll's-house! Quick, shut the door!" yelled the bear. "You dolls in the doll's-house, shut all the windows quick! Don't let that naughty mouse out!"

The curly-haired doll slammed the door of the house shut. The tiny dolls inside the house shut all the windows. Now the mouse was well and truly caught. He couldn't get out.

He went to a window and peeped out. "Where is that horrible cat?" he said, twitching his nose up and down very fast.

Nobody said a word. The mouse flew

into a rage. "I don't believe there ever
was a cat! I didn't see one! I do believe it
must have been one of you mewing, not
the cat!"

The sailor doll giggled. He really
couldn't help it. Then Bubble knew for
certain that a trick had been played on
him and he scampered up and down the
little stairs in the doll's-house, trying to
get out. But he couldn't.

What a furious rage he was in! He was so angry that he scared the little dolls and they had to get into the bedroom wardrobe to hide.

Then Alice and Ian came back into the playroom. They went to the mouse's cage and Alice gave a little scream.

"Oh no! The door of the cage is open! I do hope the mice haven't escaped."

Squeak was there of course – but Bubble wasn't. So the two children began to hunt about all over the playroom. Alice was nearly in tears.

"He was so sweet. I did love him. Oh, Bubble, where have you gone?"

Bubble heard Alice's voice and he pressed his little pink nose against a window in the doll's-house, trying to see where Alice was – and quite suddenly she saw him!

"Oh, look – isn't that Bubble in my doll's-house? Yes, it is, it is – looking out of the window. Oh, Bubble, you look sweet in there. But you must come back to your nice, safe, cosy, cage with Squeak."

The children looked at one another. "You know," said Alice, "there's something strange about this, Ian. I know the door and windows of my doll's-house were open, because I opened them myself this morning. Well then – who shut them when Bubble got in? Whoever was it that caught him there?"

They looked round at the toys, sitting so still and quiet round the playroom. Alice looked hard at the sailor doll.

"He's got a wider smile than usual on his little face!" she said. "Sailor Doll, I'm sure you caught the mouse. Thank you very much. I shall let you go home with Ian to play with his toys as a reward."

So he did, and when the sailor doll came back he had quite a few stories to tell the other toys. It was a good reward for him, wasn't it?

The
Singing Saucepan

Once upon a time there lived a pixie called Skip who made his living by selling tiny saucepans. He used to go about Fairyland, his saucepans hanging down his back on a string, their long black handles sticking out all over the place.

They were good little saucepans, and he made quite a lot of money out of them. But he was an impudent, cheeky little pixie, and many people couldn't be bothered with him. Then Skip would pull an ugly face at them and go on his way, singing a cheeky song.

One day he had sold no saucepans at all, and he was feeling very hungry.

"I really must get a penny or two somehow," he said to himself. "I am so very hungry! Ha! Here's a cottage! Perhaps the old lady who lives here will buy a saucepan."

He went up to the front door and knocked boldly.

"Who is it?" cried a voice.

"Skip, the saucepan pixie!" cried Skip. "Will you buy a fine new saucepan?"

"No," said the voice, "I don't want one. Please go away because I'm busy."

The cheeky little pixie pushed open the door and peeped in. He saw an old lady bending over her oven, looking at a fine cake she had just made. The sight made Skip's mouth water.

"Do buy one of my saucepans!" he cried.

"Didn't I tell you to go away?" said the old woman, in a temper. "Be off with you, now! I'm busy!"

"Well, cut me a slice of that cake!" said Skip.

"Certainly not!" cried the old lady. "Why, the King himself is coming to tea with me today, and I've made the cake for him!"

"Fiddlesticks!" said Skip, "I don't believe that fine tale! What, the King coming to tea with an ugly old lady like you! Never!"

That made the old woman so angry that she took up her stick, rushed at Skip, and started to chase after him. He ran out of her cottage, howling, his saucepans clanking behind him.

"The horrible old woman!" he sobbed, as he sat down behind a nearby hedge. "I'll just get my own back on her for that, I will!"

He sat and thought how he might revenge himself on the old dame, and at last he smiled a cunning smile. He took one of his saucepans and put it on the ground. Then he searched about till he found a strange little plant with a white flower and a black root. This he rubbed inside the saucepan, round and round and round, muttering magic words all the time. He stayed beneath the hedge until the afternoon, and then he peeped into the kitchen of the old lady's cottage. It was empty, for she was in her bedroom having a nap. The pixie stole in, whipped up the saucepan standing on the stove, emptied the water from it into his own saucepan, and then popped it on the stove, taking the old lady's saucepan away. Then he stole off again, hiding himself underneath the windowsill outside to watch the fun.

"When the water in my saucepan begins to boil, what a shock the old lady will get!" thought the mischievous pixie, in delight. But just then his heart nearly stopped beating for who should come driving up to the gate but the King of Fairyland himself, in a golden carriage!

"So the old lady told me the truth after all!" said the pixie, turning very pale. "How I wish I hadn't put the saucepan there with the naughty spell inside!"

He looked round to see if he could

escape, but the King's coachman was standing by the gate, and Skip did not dare to show himself. He peeped in again through the window.

The King was sitting down at the old lady's table, talking kindly to her, and eating a slice of her newly-made cake.

"This is a very nice cake," he was saying – when suddenly a loud voice began singing in the saucepan on the stove! The water was boiling, and the spell was beginning to work.

"The old woman here,
Is a miser I fear!"
sang the voice.

"She's ugly and mean,
The worst ever seen,
She's not even clean,
Her eyes they are green,
She hasn't a friend—"

The saucepan went on and on singing rude and untrue things about the surprised old dame, who couldn't think where the voice was coming from. As for the King, he stared round in astonishment, a very angry look in his eyes.

"It's the saucepan!" he cried suddenly, and ran to the stove. He lifted it off the fire, and as soon as the water went off the boil the singing voice stopped its naughty song.

"Someone's been playing a bad trick on you," he said. "Is this your saucepan?"

The old woman looked closely at it.

"No!" she said in surprise. "Oh, I know! It must belong to that saucepan pixie who wanted me to buy a saucepan from him this morning, and was very rude to me when I said I didn't want one. He must have stolen into my kitchen when I wasn't here, and popped that singing saucepan in the place of my own one. Oh, what a wicked little thing he is!"

"He shall be punished!" cried the King, in a rage, and he jumped to his feet again. At those fierce words the pixie outside the window shivered and shook from top to toe.

Then he took to his heels and ran, almost knocking down the coachman standing by the front gate.

Down the lane he tore, his saucepans clanking behind him. The coachman ran after him, but the pixie soon left him out of sight, and ran on and on for many a mile.

"I shan't be safe till I'm out of Fairy-land," he thought, as he ran. "Oh, good! There are the gates!"

He rushed out of the big golden gates, and ran on into our land till he came to a big oak-tree, under whose spreading branches he sank down to rest. His saucepans clanked loudly.

"I'd better get rid of my lovely saucepans," thought Skip, sorrowfully. "If I don't, people will easily know who I am and I might get caught and taken back to be punished."

So he stood up and shook them off his back. He looked round for somewhere to hide them. He thought that the best place would be up in the leafy greenness of the oak-tree. So he threw them all up into the tree, and then went on his way.

Where he went to, nobody knows – but the oak-tree was delighted with the tiny saucepans.

"Just the thing to sit my acorns in!" it said to itself. "Now why didn't I think of something like that before?"

So it sat each of its acorns in one of Skip's saucepans, and there they were, as safe as could be. And from that very day the oaks have always put their acorns

into little saucepans, whose handles are stuck firmly on to the twigs until the time comes for them to drop to the ground.

Have you seen them? You really must look at Skip's nice little saucepans next time you see an oak-tree!

Grandpa's Conker Tree

"Let's go and see Grandpa today, and ask him if his conker tree has thrown down the rest of its conkers for us," said Peter to Jean.

So off they went. Grandpa always saw a great deal of the children in the autumn, because they did so like picking up the satiny, brown conkers that fell from his chestnut tree.

"Aren't they lovely, Grandpa?" said Jean. "And I do like their prickly cases. Grandpa, why does the conker tree put its conkers in to such prickly green cases?"

"Well, my dear, it doesn't want its precious brown conkers eaten, that's why," said Grandpa. "Prickles always stop birds or animals from eating anything. But, as soon as the conker is ripe, and ready to root itself and grow, then down comes the case, it splits into three, and out rolls the conker."

"Grandpa, why did you plant your conker tree in a funny place?" asked Peter. "It's growing so near the wall of this shed that its branches touch it all the way up to the top."

"Well, you see – I didn't know I had planted it!" said Grandpa.

"What do you mean?" asked Jean, puzzled.

"I'll tell you about it," said Grandpa. "You know, I used to play conkers when I was a boy, just like you do. I used to choose a fine, big conker that I thought

would be the conqueror of every other boy's chestnut – and we used to hang them on strings, and hold them out for one another to hit in turn."

"Yes – we like doing that," said Peter. "I've got a conker from your tree that is a forty-fiver, Grandpa! It has smashed forty-five other conkers belonging to the boys at my school."

"Well," said Grandpa. "I once had a wonderful conker, fat and solid and strong. I put a string through it, and then I set out to make it conquer every other boy's conker."

"And did it?"

"It became a one hundred-and-sixer!" said Grandpa. "What do you think of that? And then one day I was striking another boy's conker, and my hundred-and-sixer flew off the string, shot high in the air – and disappeared!"

"Didn't you find it again?" asked Jean.

"Yes, but not until the spring!" said Grandpa. "Then I found that my hundred-and-sixer had fallen just behind the shed there – and had lain in the wet

grass, put out roots and a shoot – and grown into a beautiful little chestnut tree!"

"Oh, do conkers really grow into chestnut trees?" said Peter, surprised. "Grandpa – suppose I planted my forty-fiver?"

"Try it and see!" said Grandpa. "Maybe you will get a big chestnut tree which will throw down conkers for your grandchildren, as mine does for me! That would be fun."

So Peter is going to plant his conker and see what happens. Have you got one you can plant as well?

Mr Pink-Whistle
and Santa Claus

One night, when Mr Pink-Whistle was snoozing in front of his fire, with a big cup of cocoa at his side, he thought he heard a strange little sound. He sat up straight and listened.

Then he called Sooty his cat. "Sooty! Can you hear something – rather like a tinkling noise far away?"

Sooty popped his black head round the door. "Yes, Master – I've heard it for some time. It comes from the sky."

"Nonsense, Sooty!" said Pink-Whistle, taking a sip of his cocoa. "Surely you don't think the stars are suddenly tinkling as well as twinkling?"

Sooty laughed. "No, I don't," he said. "But it's true, Master – the sound is coming down from the sky. It's almost as if there's a tiny plane up there, going round and about looking for a landing-place, and tinkling all the time."

"Planes don't tinkle," said Pink-Whistle. "It can't be a plane! Listen – it sounds as if it's coming nearer! Let's go outside and look."

So out they went into the cold, frosty night, for it was December, and only two days before Christmas. They stood looking up into the starry sky, listening for the tinkling.

"There – I heard it again," said Sooty. "And look, Master – what's that circling round up there? It's not a plane. Whatever can it be?"

The two stared hard into the sky. They

saw a small object very high up, circling round and round. It came lower and lower – and suddenly Sooty gave a loud mew of excitement.

"Master! It's a tiny sleigh, very tiny – with one small reindeer pulling it!"

"Then it must be Santa Claus coming to pay me a visit!" Pink-Whistle said in excitement.

"No. It's not Santa Claus. It's someone small," said Sooty, who had wonderful eyesight. "Santa Claus is big and round and jolly. Look – the little sleigh is coming lower and lower."

"Get the lamp from my room and put it out here in the garden," said Pink-Whistle, excited. "Quick, Sooty!"

Soon the lamp was shining brightly in the middle of the lawn. Sooty and Pink-Whistle were glad to see that the reindeer seemed to be coming straight down to it, pulling the tiny sleigh behind him.

"Here he is! Careful, reindeer, don't knock the lamp over!" shouted Sooty. "That's right. Stand still now – you're safe."

The sleigh was indeed small – and in it sat a perky little fellow in a red tunic, cloak and feathered hat. He leaped out of the sleigh and bowed to Pink-Whistle.

"I hope I am speaking to the famous and good-hearted Mr Pink-Whistle," he said. "I have had quite a time trying to find your house. I come with a message from Santa Claus."

"Well, well, well!" said Pink-Whistle, most amazed. "How extraordinary. Please come in and have some hot cocoa."

Sooty led the way and the three of them went indoors, leaving the reindeer on the lawn trying to munch the frosty grass. Sooty fetched an old coat and threw it over him to keep him warm.

Pink-Whistle made the messenger sit down in front of the fire. He was a merry-looking fellow, and Pink-Whistle liked him. "Now," he said, "what's your message? If I can do anything for that good fellow, Santa Claus, I will. Does he want a list of children's names – children who really do deserve a lot of presents?"

"Well, no, he doesn't," said the little fellow, drinking his cocoa. "I say, isn't this good? We never have cocoa like this in Santa Claus's castle. That cat of yours

certainly knows how to make it!"

"Me-ow-ee-OW, I do know how!" said Sooty, proudly.

"Gracious – he can speak in rhyme too!" said the little fellow. "By the way, my name is Joll – short for Jolly, you know."

"It suits you," said Pink-Whistle, "but do tell me why you've come."

"Well, it's like this," said Joll. "Santa Claus is in bed with a shocking cold and cough. Good gracious, when he coughs, the whole castle shakes!"

"Goodness me – I hope he has a clever doctor," Pink-Whistle said in alarm.

"Yes, he has – so good that he won't let Santa Claus get up till next week," said Joll.

"Ah – that's very sensible," said Pink-Whistle. "He'll soon get better if he's kept in bed."

"Yes – but it's very, very awkward," said Joll. "Have you forgotten that Christmas is in two days' time – and that tomorrow night Santa Claus has to drive his sleigh and take a sack of toys to put in children's stockings? Well, how can he do that if he's in bed?"

"Oh dear – no, he can't, of course," said Pink-Whistle. "My word – whatever's to be done?"

"Aha! That's where you come in!" said Joll. "Mr Pink-Whistle, Santa Claus wants to know if you'll take his place in his sleigh on Christmas Eve? It has to be someone the children love, you see, someone they won't be scared of if they happen to see him – someone who really loves children. Well now – what about it?"

"What? Me? Me in Santa Claus's sleigh – me climbing down chimneys!" said Pink-Whistle, in amazement. "I couldn't. I don't know how to. I'd get stuck."

"No, you wouldn't," said Joll "Didn't you know that Santa Claus always sprays himself with some special magic oil, so that he can slip down any chimney, no matter how small?"

"No. No, I certainly didn't know that," said Pink-Whistle, really astonished. "But still – no, I really don't think I could drive a sleigh through the sky. I might fall out."

"I could strap you in, and come with you," said Joll. "Please do this for Santa Claus. The only other person whom we could ask would be Big-Ears, little Noddy's friend, but we really think that you would be better, because you know the children better than Big-Ears does. He lives in Toyland and knows toys better than children."

"All right. I'll do it," said Pink-Whistle, beginning to feel excited. "Yes – I'll do it!"

"Right!" said Joll, pleased. "I'll get straight back and tell Santa Claus. He'll be delighted. I'll come here on Christmas Eve and show you how to drive the

reindeer. There will be four of them. And I'll help you with the toys too, and bring the list of children."

"My word – whoever would have thought I'd take Santa Claus's place one Christmas Eve!" said Pink-Whistle, wondering if he was in a dream. "It's a great honour, Joll, a very great honour. Please tell Santa Claus I hope he'll soon be better and that I'll do my best."

"Can I come too?" asked Sooty, who had been listening in great excitement. But nobody answered him. Pink-Whistle was showing Joll out of the door, and thanking him for coming.

He watched Joll jump into the sleigh and shake the reins – and then up into the sky they went, the bells jingling merrily.

"Isn't it exciting, Sooty?" said Pink-Whistle, coming indoors, all smiles.

"You'll have to wear a very thick coat, Master," said Sooty. "It will be very, very cold driving in a sleigh up in the wintry sky."

"I haven't got a very thick coat," said

Pink-Whistle. "But never mind. I'll feel so excited that I shan't notice the cold. I'm sorry you can't come, Sooty. There wouldn't be room for you in the sleigh. My word – what an adventure I'm going to have!"

On Christmas Eve, Sooty's sharp ears once more heard the sound of bells far away in the sky. He ran to the window. "Quick! Joll's coming!" he said. "Put on your coat, Master. See – down comes the big sleigh – with four fine reindeer tossing their antlers!"

There came a knock at the door, and there stood Joll, beaming all over his face. He carried a red cloak and hood over his arm.

"Ready?" he said. "I've brought you Santa Claus's cloak to wear – it's so bitterly cold up in the sky tonight. And here's the list of children."

"Oh – I don't want to wear a cloak and hood," said Pink-Whistle. "Children might think I'm Santa Claus, and I'm not. I don't even have a beard!"

"Master, you must wear the warm cloak," said Sooty, "and take a hot-water bottle for your feet. I don't want to have you in bed with a cough and cold for weeks!"

"All right, all right," said Pink-Whistle, in a grumbly voice. "I'll wear the cloak – but I won't wear the hood, I shall wear my own hat – and I certainly shan't take a hot-water bottle for my feet."

"Come along, quickly, or we'll be late," said Joll, and he put the red cloak round Pink-Whistle's shoulders. "Keep your hat on if you want to – but hold on to it when the wind blows!"

Jingle-jingle-jingle – the sleigh rose into the air pulled by the four excited reindeer. Joll drove them for some way,

then handed the reins to Pink-Whistle, who found that he could drive four lively reindeer quite easily. My word – how the wind streaked past his nose, and how glad he was that his hat was jammed on his head so tightly. He was cold even in the thick red cloak – and as for his feet, they were like ice!

"I wish I had brought a hot-water bottle for them, after all," he said. And even as he said that he felt a slow, cosy warmth settling on his feet. "Magic!" he thought. "I wished for a hot-water bottle and it came! Well, well, I am enjoying this!"

It was most exciting to land gently on rooftops, beside tall chimneys, and even more exciting to find how easy it was to slip down them, once Joll had sprayed him with the magic oil! Pink-Whistle slid down each chimney as easily as a snake, and landed in bedroom after bedroom, where sleeping children lay dreaming of the presents they would find next morning.

"It's nice to fill stockings," thought Pink-Whistle. "I'll put an engine into this stocking – and a doll into that – and where's that little car? Here it is. And there's a book as well. Dear me, how excited these sleeping children will be tomorrow morning."

I can't tell you how many stockings Pink-Whistle filled that Christmas Eve, nor how many sleeping children he saw. All but one were sound asleep – one small boy woke up as Pink-Whistle landed on the hearth-rug in his bedroom. How he stared when he saw someone he thought was Santa Claus – wearing a top hat!

"You're not Santa Claus," he said. "Where's your beard? And why haven't you a hood instead of a hat? I'll shout and call my mother!"

Well, Pink-Whistle disappeared up that chimney at lightning speed! Good gracious! He didn't want to face an angry mother! When he sat panting on the roof he remembered that he hadn't had time to fill the boy's stocking. So he carefully dropped a few toys down the chimney, hoping they would land safely on the hearth-rug. Then he scrambled into the sleigh beside Joll, and away he went.

"Well, I did enjoy that!" he said, when it was all over, and he was safely driving home in the sleigh, his feet being warmed again by what felt like a nice warm and furry hot-water bottle. "Please thank Santa Claus for giving me the chance of visiting the children on Christmas Eve, Joll. It was wonderful! Oh – here we are on my lawn again. Like a nice hot drink?"

"No thanks," said Joll. "I must go and report to Santa Claus. He'll be longing to know if everything went off all right."

"Well – I'll go and report to Sooty, my cat, too," said Pink-Whistle, getting out of the sleigh, and going to pat the reindeer, and give them a lump of sugar each.

"Oh – Sooty knows all about your exciting evening," said Joll, with a chuckle. "He stowed himself away under the rug; didn't you know? He was your hot-water bottle, Mr Pink-Whistle, and curled himself up on your feet to keep them warm! Come out, Sooty, you rascal!"

And out leaped Sooty, and rubbed himself against Pink-Whistle. "I enjoyed it all too!" he said. "Now let's go in and have a hot drink, Master, and talk about our wonderful evening!"

They stood and waved goodbye to Joll and the fine reindeer. The bells sounded more and more faintly, and then died away.

"You're a naughty cat, Sooty," said Pink-Whistle, when they were sitting drinking hot lemon by the warm fire. "But I must say you were a very good hot-water bottle! Listen – one little boy was awake and saw me. I'm afraid he'll never believe in Santa Claus again, because he saw my top hat."

"Well, he'll believe in *you* all right!" said Sooty. "Let's have this exciting evening put into a story, Master – and then when the boy reads it, he'll know that he was the only child in the world who saw you instead of Santa Claus this Christmas Eve! How surprised he must have been to see someone coming down the chimney in a top hat!"

I must say I'd have been surprised too – but I'd have known it was kind old Pink-Whistle, wouldn't you?

Policeman
Billy

There was once a small boy called Billy, who loved dressing up. One birthday he was very pleased because his Uncle Jim gave him a set of policeman's clothes! They were just big enough for him. There was a blue tunic, a belt and a fine plastic helmet which looked just like the one a real policeman would have.

"Ooh!" said Billy in delight. "Just exactly what I wanted! Now I can dress up and pretend to be a policeman!"

"Here's a pencil and a notebook for you," said his father. "If you're going to be a policeman you must have those. You can write down things about the people you see then. You never know when your notes will come in useful!"

Billy was so pleased. He was soon

dressed in his policeman's uniform, and very smart he looked, I can tell you! It was a pity there were no trousers to go with it, because Billy felt that his shorts didn't look exactly right with the uniform – but that couldn't be helped!

"I will pretend there are robbers up on the common," said Billy to his mother. "I am going up there with my notebook. I'll hide under a bush and make notes about all the people going by, in case they happen to be my pretend robbers!"

His mother laughed, "Run along, then!" she said. "I hope you'll be a successful policeman!"

Billy ran off, proud to be dressed in a policeman's blue uniform, helmet and all! He had his notebook and pencil in his pocket. What a fine game he was going to have!

He was soon up on the common. It was a fine day and the sun shone down hotly. Billy found a bush and sat underneath it, waiting for people to come by, for the road was quite near. But very soon he felt too hot. His helmet seemed very heavy, but he couldn't bear to take it off. Besides, he was quite sure that a real policeman would have to keep it on.

Not far off was a little broken-down shed. Billy thought he would go and hide there. It would be cooler in the shed than outside on the common. He could easily peep through a crack in the wooden walls and see who passed by.

He ran to the shed. It was very dark inside, for the only window was very small indeed, and it was so dirty that hardly any light came through at all. At one end of the shed there was a crack in the wooden wall, and Billy sat down on

some sacks and put his eye to the crack.
He could see the road quite well from
there. He took out his notebook. He could
only just see to write in it! He put the
date, and the place where he was, and
then he began to wait patiently.

Soon Mr Straws the farmer came by on
his tractor. Billy wrote down: *At a quarter
past 10 saw Mr Straws on his tractor,
wearing old brown jacket and no cap.*
After that Mrs Lane went by on her
bicycle. Billy entered her into his book
too: *At half past 10 Mrs Lane went by on
bicycle, wearing blue skirt, blue jumper
and black hat. She had a big hole in the
back of her right stocking.*

"I would make a good real policeman, I'm sure," thought Billy to himself, as he wrote. "I do notice things. Daddy says that's one of the first things a policeman learns to do – to notice even little things."

After that no one came by for a long time. Billy felt sleepy. It was fun to be a policeman, but a bit boring when nothing much happened. Also it was rather smelly in the shed.

Then he heard the noise of a car. He put his eye to the crack and looked through. He saw that a dark blue car was coming slowly along. The man at the wheel was alone. He seemed to be looking out for something. Just as Billy was writing down: *At ¼ past 11 a dark blue saloon car came by, number GHR 419, with one man* . . . the car stopped. Billy peeped again. The man looked quickly all round him and then took a bundle out of the car. He ran swiftly over the common to the shed where Billy was. But he didn't go inside. He went to the back of it where he could not be seen from the road. Billy was astonished. He sat still for a minute and wondered what to do. What would a real policeman do? Well, a real policeman would find out what the man was doing and put it all down, he was sure. Billy got up and went to the other side of the shed to find a crack that he could look through. He soon found one and peeped out.

The man was there – and he was behaving very strangely! He had taken off his coat and shirt and was busy putting on a brown jersey, and a brown coat over that! He threw his cap into a bush and put on a hat instead. Then he

did something very peculiar indeed! He took a little black thing out of a pocket and stuck it firmly on his top lip.

"Gosh, he's given himself a moustache!" thought Billy, amazed. "Whatever can he be doing all that for? Is he playing a game of pretend like me? Well I'd better write all this down, I think. It's very exciting."

So he wrote in his notebook: *The man hid at back of shed, and changed his clothes. He threw his old clothes into a big gorse bush nearby. He put on a brown jersey and a brown coat, and grey hat. He also put on a little black moustache. The man was small and had one of his thumbs bandaged up. His nose was a bit crooked. I couldn't see the colour of his eyes, but his hair was red-brown.*

The man looked all round him once more, saw that no one was coming and ran back to his car. He jumped into it and off he went at top speed. Billy wrote again in his notebook: *The man got into the car and drove off fast towards Winter Hill.*

After that nobody else came at all for a whole hour. It was very boring. Billy nearly went to sleep. He did wish something else exciting would happen, like that man who came and changed his clothes.

Suddenly Billy saw two real policemen driving slowly up the road, in a police car. They stopped not far off, got out of the car and sat down on a seat by the side of the road. Billy thought he would go and talk to them. Whatever would they say when they saw a small, dressed-up policeman like himself! He ran out of the shed and went up to them immediately.

"Hello, who's this!" said one of the policemen, with a grin. "Good morning, Inspector!"

"Good morning, sir!" said the other policeman taking out his notebook and pretending to look through it very solemnly, shaking his head. "What about you, Inspector?" he said to Billy, shutting his notebook with a snap. "Have you anything to report? Or perhaps you don't keep a notebook?"

"Of course I do!" said Billy indignantly. "And I'd say mine's a nicer notebook than yours, too! I've written quite a lot in it this morning."

"Let me see," said the first policeman grinning, and he held out his hand. Billy gave him the notebook and the policeman turned over the pages, reading all about Mr Straws going by in his tractor, and about Mrs Lane and the hole in her stocking.

But when he came to the big piece about the man in the car, the policeman stopped smiling. He read it all through very carefully, and then passed the book over to his companion.

"Read that!" he said. "What do you make of it?" Then he turned to Billy.

112

"Did you make all that up?" he asked. "Or did it really happen?"

"Of course it happened!" said Billy. "I can show you where the old clothes are, in a big gorse bush."

Both policemen sprang to their feet. Billy showed them where the man had thrown the clothes, and they pulled them out quickly.

"Good grief, it must have been Sid Brown who pulled off the robbery last night!" said the first policeman. "We must go back to the station, Ted. We'll catch him now we know what he's dressed like – a moustache and all, too – and a bandaged thumb! We'll soon have him! Come on, sonny, jump in the back of the car and we'll take you with us!"

So, still dressed in his policeman's uniform, Billy, tremendously excited, rode in the back of the police car all the way to the police station. There they saw a real

inspector, who solemnly read Billy's notebook, gave a lot of sharp orders, asked Billy a good many questions and then made a lot of phone calls.

It was near Billy's lunch-time and he felt hungry. "Could I go home now?" he asked. "My mother will be wondering where I am."

"Yes, you can go off duty, Inspector!" said the real inspector, beaming at Billy. "You've done well today, young man – we shall catch a thief who's been worrying us for a long time!"

Billy tore off in delight. But when he got home and told his mother and father they laughed at him.

"You're making it all up, Billy!" said his mother and they simply would not believe him when he said it was all quite true – he had seen the man, he had seen the policemen, he had been to the police station, and he had helped to catch a real thief!

But his parents soon changed their minds when a big policeman came to the house that evening and told them that,

thanks to Billy's notebook, they had managed to catch Sid Brown, the clever thief! How pleased and proud they were!

"So you *were* a real policeman today!" said his mother, hugging him. "And not a pretend one!"

The next week a parcel came for Billy. Inside was – what do you think? A fine policeman's whistle, and a policeman's waterproof cape, made just the right size! The note with it said: *For Chief Inspector Billy – with compliments from Chief Inspector Rawlings.*

Wasn't Billy proud! Well – you should just see him all dressed up now, cape, whistle and all, just like a real policeman!

Mr
Do-As-I-Like

Everyone called him Do-As-I-Like, because he always said "I do as I like" – and what is more, he did! He was a vain little bully of a goblin, bad tempered and tiresome. How everyone hated him!

One day he met little Mr Smarty. Mr Smarty was a goblin, too, and today he was dressed in his best clothes.

"Oho!" said Mr Do-As-I-Like, standing in front of him. "You're looking very, very smart today, Smarty. I hear you've got a shop. What about taking me there and dressing me from top to toe? I could do with a new suit, some shoes and a hat."

"Er – well – I am in a bit of a hurry today, Do-As-I-Like," said Mr Smarty, as he tried to edge away.

"Are you? Well, so am I," said Mr Do-

As-I-Like. "Come on – let's hurry along to your shop, Smarty. I'm going to a grand party tomorrow, and I want to look nice. I'll have a fine top hat, and a red suit and a pair of red shoes, and . . ."

"But – but – you won't find—" began poor Smarty. Mr Do-As-I-Like stopped him.

"Now, no excuses! Take me straight along to your shop. Do you want me to turn you into a worm and tread on you?"

"No! Oh, no, no!" cried poor Mr Smarty. "Come with me. You shall have a wonderful new set of clothes, just for the taking, Do-As-I-Like!"

"Aha! That sounds more like it," said Mr Do-As-I-Like, and followed Mr Smarty at once. They came to a big street. On the corner was an enormous shop, whose windows were filled with lovely clothes. Mr Do-As-I-Like was most impressed. "Wonderful!" he said. "Beautiful shop you've got, Smarty. Come along in."

"You go first," said Mr Smarty, politely. He opened the door for him. He followed

Mr Do-As-I-Like into the shop, and pointed up the stairs.

"Up there," he said. "Pray help yourself to anything you want. Don't bother to be polite to anyone. Just take what you like and do what you like."

"I shall," said Mr Do-As-I-Like, grandly, and he walked up the stairs. He came to another part of the shop where all kinds of clothes were set out. Mr Do-As-I-Like saw a fine red suit. He pulled it down at once and began to try it on. It fitted him well.

An assistant came up. "Can I help you, sir?" he said.

"Yes, get me three more suits like this, one in blue, one in yellow and one in green," said Mr Do-As-I-Like, haughtily. "And look sharp about it. And get me top hats to match and shoes as well. I really don't care a fig about the price."

Of course he didn't. He expected Mr Smarty to pay for it all!

Soon he had a great array of clothes, and he ordered the assistant to pack them all up for him to take away.

"There is your bill, sir," said the assistant, handing him the enormous parcel of clothes.

"Mr Smarty will pay," said Mr Do-As-I-Like.

"Who's he?" said the assistant, looking puzzled.

"Well, he owns this shop, silly," said Mr Do-As-I-Like.

"But this is Mr Bom-Bom's shop," said the assistant, looking even more puzzled. "I'll call him."

Mr Bom-Bom came. He was a tall,

burly gnome, with very sharp eyes indeed. "What's all this?" he said. "This is my shop, it doesn't belong to anyone called Smarty! You will please pay the bill or I shall call Mr Plod the policeman."

"B-B-But – Mr Smarty himself brought me here!" stammered Mr Do-As-I-Like in amazement. "He opened the door for me – told me to go upstairs and choose what I liked."

"The only Smarty I know is Mr Smarty who owns the fish-shop," said Mr Bom-Bom, looking very fierce. "He has shut up his shop today, and dressed himself in his best to go to his niece's wedding. And what is your name?"

"Mr Do-As-I-Like," said the goblin in a very small voice.

"Hmmm! I thought so," said Mr Bom-Bom. "Well, what about my bill? Or shall we call in Mr Plod the policeman and ask him to settle the matter for us?"

So Mr Do-As-I-Like had to pay, and spend nearly all his money.

"All these fine clothes, and not even enough left to buy a few sausages for my supper!" he groaned. "Wait till I meet Mr Smarty again. Just wait!"

But when he passed Mr Smarty's fish-shop the next day, and saw the little fishmonger grinning to himself, he decided not to say a word to him at all.

No – if Mr Smarty could play a trick like that once, he might well think up another. It did serve Mr Do-As-I-Like right, didn't it?

What's Happened
to the Clock?

Patsy and William were busy putting out their railway on the playroom floor. It took a long time because there were so many rails to fit together, and some of them were rather difficult.

"After we've put all the rails out, we'll put up the signals, and the station, and the tunnel," said Patsy. "Isn't it a beautiful railway set, William?"

It certainly was. It had belonged to their Uncle Ronnie, and he had gone abroad and had given them the set he had had when he was a boy. He had looked after it carefully and everything was as good as new.

At last all the rails were fitted together, the station was put up, with little porters and passengers standing on the platform, and the tunnel was placed over one part of the line.

"Now for the signals, and then we can put the engine on the lines with the carriages and set it going," said William.

Patsy looked at the clock to see what time it was. She gave a cry. "Oh, dear! Just look at the time. It's only five minutes to our bedtime – and we've just come to the very nicest part of all – getting the train going!"

William frowned. "This bedtime business! We always seem to have to go to bed just when we're in the middle of something exciting. Yesterday we had to go before we finished the pictures we were painting."

"And the night before that I couldn't finish the story I was reading," said Patsy. "Bother the clock. It goes much too fast."

"What's Mum doing?" said William suddenly.

"She's turning out the old chests on the landing," said Patsy, looking surprised. "Why?"

"Well – she won't guess how the time is

going, then," said William, and he got up from the floor. He went to the clock and turned the hands so that instead of saying a quarter past seven, they said a quarter past six!

"There!" said William. "It's only a quarter past six. We've got another hour to play!"

"Oh, William!" said Patsy, shocked. "You can't do a thing like that."

"Well, I have," said William. "Mum isn't wearing her watch today because the glass is broken and it's at the jeweller's. She'll come and look at this clock – and she'll think it's right – so then we'll have a whole hour extra to play in!"

Patsy didn't say any more. She wanted the extra hour. Perhaps their mother would never guess!

Mother called from the landing after a while. "Surely it is getting near your bedtime, you two. What does the clock say?"

William looked at it. "Twenty-five to seven," he called.

"Really? But surely it is later than that?" said Mother. She popped her head in at the door and stared hard at the clock. "Dear me – how extraordinary. It does say twenty-five to seven. Has it stopped?"

"No, it hasn't," said William not looking at his mother. He suddenly felt rather ashamed. Patsy did too. She turned very red in the face and her mother wondered why.

"Well – I suppose I must have mistaken the time," said Mother, and went to get on with her turning-out. The children didn't say anything to one another. They both wished they hadn't put the clock back like that – they had tricked their mother, and that was a horrible thing to do.

"Do you think we ought to tell Mummy what we've done?" asked Patsy, after a time.

"No," said William. "We've done it and we might as well take the extra hour."

So they didn't say a word to their mother. They went to bed at quarter past eight instead of quarter past seven,

feeling rather tired – though the clock, of course, only showed quarter past seven!

Next morning the clock appeared to be quite right again. When the children heard the eight o'clock hooter going, far away in the town, the clock said eight o'clock too. How had it got itself right again? They looked at Mother, wondering if she would say anything about it, but she didn't say a word.

They went to school as usual, stayed there to lunch, and came back to tea. They did their homework and then went up to the playroom to go on playing with their railway. It looked very exciting indeed, all set out there.

"I'll have one engine and you have the other," said William. They were lucky because there were two engines, and it was fun to set them both going and switch them from one line to another just when it seemed as if there was going to be a collision.

They had played for what seemed a very short time, when Mummy put her head round the door.

"Not much more time," she said. "Make the best of what time is left before going to bed."

The children were astonished. Why, surely it couldn't be more than six o'clock! They had hardly played any time at all! They glanced at the clock.

"Why – it says five past seven!" cried Patsy. "It can't be five past seven. It simply can't."

"No, it can't," said William. But certainly the clock said five past seven. "Shall I alter it again?" he asked.

"No – don't," said Patsy at once. "For one thing, Mummy has seen the time – and for another, I don't want to trick her again. I felt dreadful about that. I think we ought to have owned up when she came to kiss us goodnight – and we didn't."

They argued about the time for a while, then Mother called from the bathroom. "What's the time by the clock, children? Surely it's bedtime now?"

They looked at the clock. It said a quarter past seven.

"Mum, the clock says a quarter past seven," called William. "But it can't be! What's happened to the clock? I'm sure it isn't right."

"Dear me – a quarter past seven already," said their mother. "Well, you must certainly go to bed then. Just tidy up quickly and come along. You can leave your rails out, of course."

So the children had to leave their railway before they had set the engines going for more than once or twice round the rails. It was very disappointing.

They had their baths, brushed their teeth and hair, and got into bed. Mother said she would bring them some hot chocolate.

While they were sitting up in bed, still feeling gloomy, William heard the church clock beginning to strike. He listened and counted.

"One-two-three-four-five-six-seven – why, it only struck seven times. It's seven o'clock, not eight o'clock."

"We've come to bed a whole hour early," said Patsy.

"Mum!" called William. "The church clock has just struck seven. It isn't eight o'clock. It's seven. We've missed a whole hour's play."

"The playroom clock says eight o'clock," said Mother. "You went by that yesterday, didn't you? – so you must go by it today."

Mother sounded rather stern. Patsy looked at her and burst into tears. "Mummy! We put the clock back yesterday so that we could have a whole hour's extra play. We were horrible!"

"Yes, it was rather horrible," said Mother. "I really thought it was just a trick and that you'd own up, you know, when I kissed you goodnight. Then I saw that you really did mean to deceive me. And now the clock has paid you back! It's an hour before its time instead of an hour after."

"Mum," said William, "I believe you've played a trick, haven't you? If you haven't, what's happened to the clock?"

"Of course I've played a trick," said Mother, laughing. "Exactly the same trick that you played me, but the other way round. Now drink your chocolate and go to sleep."

"Mummy, I'm very sorry," said Patsy,

rubbing her eyes. "I felt quite dreadful about it. I'm glad you played a trick too – now we're quits!"

"Yes – we're quits!" said Mother, and she kissed her and William, too. "You gained an hour and lost an hour and perhaps learned a lesson – so we won't say any more about it."

They didn't – and you won't be surprised to hear that the playroom clock has behaved in quite an ordinary way ever since!

Mr Binkle's
Boots

Mr Binkle was a fat brownie who lived in the corner cottage in the village of Fuff. He was fat because he ate such a lot, and he ate such a lot because he was rich and could buy plenty of food.

But although he was rich, he was a mean, stingy fellow who never gave a penny away, and wouldn't dream of putting down a saucer of milk for a stray cat. If a beggar came to the door he slammed it in his face and let his dog loose. He was not a very kind brownie, and the people in the village of Fuff didn't like him at all.

Mr Binkle was very friendly with His Highness, Prince Mighty, who lived in Twinkling Palace on the hill beyond the village. Prince Mighty liked Mr Binkle because he flattered him so much.

"You are the handsomest prince in the world, Your Highness!" Mr Binkle would say. "You are the most powerful prince and the greatest ruler!"

This was all nonsense, because Prince Mighty was an ugly little fellow, and as for being powerful, well, he couldn't even manage his own servants. He had no kingdom to rule over except for his palace grounds, and even they were not very big!

But he believed everything that Mr Binkle said and liked to have him to tea to hear all the nice things that the artful brownie was ready to tell him.

Mr Binkle was very proud of his friendship with Prince Mighty, and he wouldn't be friends with anyone else in Fuff. Not that anyone cared, for everybody thought he was a horrible little man, and laughed at him behind his back. Mr Binkle always looked down his nose when he met anyone in the village, and wouldn't even say good morning. So nobody said good morning to him.

One day Prince Mighty asked Mr Binkle to go to lunch with him at one o'clock. This was the first time he had been asked to lunch and the brownie was most excited.

"I must have a new suit!" he thought. "I must have a new hat! I must have new shoes!"

He went to the pixie tailor, and to the gnome shoemaker. He ordered a wonderful suit of yellow silk with gold buttons down the front and a blue satin cloak to go over his shoulders. He ordered a pair of blue shoes with long, pointed toes, and then he went to the pixie hatter's and bought a marvellous hat. It was yellow and had seven little points with bells on each. It made a lovely ringing noise, and Mr Binkle was thoroughly delighted with it.

"How smart I shall be!" he said to himself, when all the things he ordered had been sent home. He laid them out on the bed and looked at them.

"Prince Mighty will be quite jealous of me!" he thought. "Ha-ha! What a fine time I shall have walking down the village street with everyone staring at my fine new suit of clothes!"

When the great day came Mr Binkle had a big disappointment. The rain was pouring down, and the streets were running with water. There was mud everywhere, and Mr Binkle looked at his new shoes in dismay. They were not meant for walking through mud.

"Perhaps it will clear up before it is time to go," he said, and he stood at the window to watch.

Presently the rain stopped and the sun came out. "Hurrah!" said Mr Binkle. "I shall be all right now! Except for my shoes, of course – now what can I do about them? I really can't walk through the muddy fields in these beautiful new shoes. I must put them safely in a bag and wear my boots."

But when he went to get his boots he found that one of them had a large hole underneath that let the water in. Mr Binkle always caught a cold when his feet got wet and he didn't know what to do. And just as he was wondering, there came a knock at the door.

"The baker," said Mr Binkle to himself, and went to see. But it wasn't the baker. It was a funny old lady, dressed in a raggedy shawl and a pointed hat. She was holding up her yellow skirt out of the wet, and on her feet she wore a fine pair of high rubber boots.

"Good morning," she said, politely. "Could you give me a crust of bread? I haven't had anything to eat since yesterday."

"I don't like beggars," said Mr Binkle, crossly. "Go away! I shan't give you anything at all."

"Just a drink of water, then," said the old woman. "That won't cost you anything."

"No," said Mr Binkle, in his meanest voice. "I pump my own water and I don't give it away to beggars. Go away!"

The old woman hitched up her skirts, and walked down the garden path, mumbling to herself. As she went Mr Binkle caught sight of her rubber boots, and an idea came to him.

"Hey!" he called. "Come back! Come back!"

The old woman came back, and stood at the door again.

"I'll buy those boots from you," said Mr Binkle, pointing to them. "I'll give you a piece of chicken pie and a drink of milk."

140

"No," said the old dame. "They cost a lot of money. You give me some money and then you shall have them."

"How much money?" asked Mr Binkle.

"Ten silver coins," said the old woman. Mr Binkle laughed loudly although he knew that they would be cheap for only ten silver coins.

"Fiddlesticks!" he said. "What nonsense! Why, they're not even worth five! And I don't expect they would fit me, anyhow."

The old dame was hungry and she wanted something to eat. So she slipped off her boots and told Mr Binkle to try them. They fitted him perfectly! He

meant to have them, and he wondered how he could get them for very little money.

"I'll get you the chicken pie and the milk," he said, "and you shall have my old boots to go off in instead of walking barefoot. And I'll give you a silver coin into the bargain!"

"No," said the old dame crossly. "That's not enough. Give me nine silver coins, the pie and your old boots. Then you shall have my nice new ones."

"What, do you dare to argue with me?" cried Mr Binkle, pretending to be angry. "I'll set the dog on you!"

The old woman looked at him. It was a strange look and Mr Binkle felt a shiver go down his back. Suppose the old dame was a witch? Then he laughed scornfully, and went to his larder. He picked up half of a chicken pie, and a small bottle of milk, and went into the hall. He told the woman to put on his boots and he gave her one silver coin.

"Here you are," he said. "Now be off with you! I've treated you very well."

"I tell you I want my boots back," said the old woman, angrily. "I don't want this pie and only one silver coin. And as for these old boots of yours, they're not even worth a penny, for they let the water in at the bottom."

Mr Binkle pushed her out of the door, and then he pointed to the kennel where Snarly, his dog, lived. "Go away quickly," he said, "or I will set Snarly free."

The old woman was afraid of dogs, and mumbling and grumbling she ran down the garden path in Mr Binkle's old boots. When she got to the gate she looked back with a very strange sparkle in her eyes. She muttered a few words in a low voice and then went down the street. Ah, Mr Binkle, what magic words those were that you didn't hear!

Mr Binkle was delighted with himself and the rubber boots. Now he could go through the fields safely, and take his new shoes with him in a bag. He could change into them at the palace and arrive in Prince Mighty's dining-room looking just as smart as smart could be!

He dressed himself in his yellow tunic, his blue cloak, his seven-pointed hat with the bells ringing merrily, and put his blue shoes in a bag.

Then he started off for the palace, singing a happy little song, and hoping that everybody in Fuff village would see him as he passed by.

But what a funny thing! When he got to the gate of his cottage the rubber boots suddenly became very tight, for all the world as if they were holding his feet and not meaning to let them go. And then they started to play tricks on Mr Binkle!

First they walked his feet to an extra large puddle and jumped right in! *Splash!* The water soaked his tunic and splashed his fine cloak. Mr Binkle was horrified. Whatever was happening? He hadn't meant to walk into that puddle and yet he had gone there. What a very peculiar thing!

Soon the boots walked him to a ditch full of black mud. They jumped into it, and of course poor Mr Binkle had to go too! *Splitter-splutter-splash!* Black mud flew into the air and a large drop went into Mr Binkle's eye. Another drop ran down his fat nose and made him look very comical. As for his poor cloak, it was running with black mud!

"Good gracious me, what a terrible thing this is," said Mr Binkle, almost crying. "These boots must be bewitched. I must take them off before they do any more damage."

He sat down on a post and tried to pull them off, but he couldn't. They held tightly to his feet, and no matter how he pulled they wouldn't budge an inch. At last he gave it up, and looked sadly at his spoilt tunic.

"I must go home," he said. "I shall have to change into my other clothes, for these are quite spoiled. I don't know what the prince would say if I went to lunch with him wearing these muddy things."

He got up to go back to his cottage – but the boots had quite other ideas. No, they wanted to go somewhere else, and to Mr Binkle's horror they walked up the path in Mrs Dibble-Dabble's backyard and went right to her big dog's kennel. The dog growled and showed his teeth. Mr Binkle wanted to run away but he couldn't. Oh my, what a dreadful thing it was!

The dog suddenly growled again, and one of the boots tapped him on the nose. The dog rushed at Mr Binkle and bit a piece out of his blue cloak. Then he growled at the mischievous boots, and they decided it was time to go away.

Down the path they went, and Mrs Dibble-Dabble looked out of the window and shouted, "It serves you right, Mr Binkle, for teasing my dog!"

He hadn't a moment to explain, for the boots ran him down the road to where a big tabby cat was lying asleep on a warm patch of sand. The boots trod on her tail, and the cat woke up with a hiss, flew at Mr Binkle and scratched his right hand. Then it tore a hole in his tunic, and Mr Binkle could have cried with dismay.

"You hateful boots!" he said. "You hateful boots! If only I could take you off, I'd throw you into the nearest pool!"

The boots were having the time of

their life! The old dame had put a spell on them and they were enjoying their pranks tremendously. What would they do next?

Aha! Look, there was Mr Ding-Dong the gnome sitting asleep on the seat in front of his house. His feet were stretched out in front of him, and the boots thought it would be great fun to tread on them. Mr Binkle guessed what they were going to do when he felt them taking him towards Ding-Dong, and he was afraid. Ding-Dong was a bad-tempered gnome, and there was no knowing what he might do.

The boots cared nothing for Mr Binkle's fears. They ran up to Ding-Dong and trod hard on his outstretched feet.

"Ooh!" Ding-Dong the gnome woke up with a shout. When he saw that it was Mr Binkle who had trodden on his toes he was very angry indeed. Out went his right hand and slapped Mr Binkle's left cheek, and out went his left hand and slapped Mr Binkle's right cheek. *Slap! Slap!* Just like that. Mr Binkle gave a

howl and tried to run away, but the boots held him there.

"Don't slap me again," he begged. "I didn't mean any harm. These boots of mine are bewitched, and made me tread on your toes."

"What a silly story!" said Ding-Dong, scornfully. "Be off with you, or I'll slap you again."

Fortunately the boots decided that they would go on their way again, so off they started. To Mr Binkle's dismay they took the path that led to the palace of Prince Mighty. Surely they were not going to take him there? Why, he was in a dreadful state and the prince would be disgusted with him.

Yes, sure enough the boots were going to the palace, but on the way there they walked into every ditch, puddle and pond they came across, and poor Mr Binkle became blacker and muddier and wetter and more ragged with every step.

At last the boots walked him through the palace gate. The guard tried to stop Mr Binkle, but it was no use, the boots took him on. In through the palace door he walked, and dear me, right into the prince's dining-room! It was half past one, and the prince was looking as black as thunder, for Mr Binkle was half an hour late. He was eating his lunch alone when the brownie came into the room, leaving great black footprints behind him wherever he went.

The prince jumped up angrily and demanded to know who Mr Binkle was, for he did not recognise the brownie in his dirty, muddy state, his face dirty and his hair wet.

"I'm Binkle," said the brownie, almost crying.

"BINKLE!" said the prince in

amazement and anger. "How dare you come here in this state! Why, you look like a chimney-sweep – and half an hour late, too! How dare you, I say!"

Mr Binkle was just going to explain that it was all the fault of the boots when they started dancing. Oh dear me, how they kicked into the air and tap-tapped on the floor, making Mr Binkle so out of breath that he couldn't say a word, because of course he had to dance too! Prince Mighty watched him in the greatest astonishment, growing more and more angry.

"Stop!" he said. "Stop! This is a rude and unseemly thing to do! You arrive here late, and in a dirty suit, and instead of saying you are sorry you start to dance all over my new carpet in your horrible boots!"

The boots were cross to hear themselves called horrible, and they danced up to Prince Mighty and trod on his toes. Then they kicked him hard, though Mr Binkle tried his very hardest to stop them.

"BINKLE!" roared the prince in the biggest, angriest voice he had. "How dare you! I'll have you locked up in a dungeon! Are you mad?"

The boots really were enjoying themselves. They suddenly jumped up on the table and began to dance among the dishes, and whenever they came to a salt-cellar, mustard pot, rolls of bread or napkin rings they kicked them right off the table! Mr Binkle was simply horrified, but he had to go up on the table with the boots, and it looked for all the world as if it were he who was doing all these wicked things.

Prince Mighty rolled up his sleeves and ran at Mr Binkle. He pushed him right in the middle of the chest and the brownie was flung off the table and landed in a corner.

"Ooh! Don't!" he cried, the tears running down his cheeks. "I tell you it's the boots that are doing all this, not me!"

But Prince Mighty just didn't believe him.

"Boots, is it?" he said, scornfully. "But whose legs are inside the boots, making them dance and kick, that's what I'd like to know! Boots indeed!"

He came up to Mr Binkle to push him again, and he looked so fierce that even the boots were frightened.

They jumped Mr Binkle to his feet and began to run away. They could run very

fast indeed, and they were soon out of the palace and running down the steps with poor Mr Binkle panting loudly. The Prince saw that he couldn't catch him, so, taking a handful of squashy tomatoes off the dining-table he hurled them with all his might at the unhappy brownie.

Splosh! Splosh! They hit Mr Binkle at the back of the neck, and burst all over his cloak. The boots hurried along, and not until they were well out of reach of the prince and his guards did they go more slowly.

But by now the magic was wearing out, and not much was left. They took Mr Binkle right through the village of Fuff, and he was terribly ashamed when everyone came out to look at him.

"Ho! Look at old Mr Binkle!" cried all the people, in delighted surprise. "Isn't he a sight! Ha-ha! Ho-ho!"

Mr Binkle blushed red, and wished the boots would hurry along – but the magic was almost gone, and the boots went very slowly indeed, quite tired out. At last they reached the corner cottage where the brownie lived, and walked slowly up the path. Mr Binkle sat down in the hall and looked at them. They were no longer holding his feet tightly, and he wondered if he could take them off.

He tried. They came off quite easily, and he heard them sigh when he tossed them into a corner. They could do no more mischief. The magic had all gone.

Mr Binkle sighed too. He took off his dirty, wet clothes and turned the water on to have a bath. Then he got into the hot water and lay down to soak off all the mud. And he began to think hard.

"Prince Mighty will never be friends with me again," he thought. "And the people of Fuff will laugh whenever they see me, especially when they hear all that the boots made me do. They will say that the old dame did right to put a spell on the boots, because I was so mean to her.

"Well," said Mr Binkle honestly to himself, "I was mean. When I think about myself, I see that I am a proud, stuck-up, mean, stingy fellow. Nobody likes me, and I've a good mind to pack up my things and go where nobody knows me.

"But, no – I won't. That wouldn't be at all a brave thing to do. I shall stay here, and if people point their fingers at me and laugh, I will say, 'Yes, laugh at me. I deserve it.' I shall stay here and try to be different."

He did stay, and he did try. Of course everyone pointed their fingers at him, and Prince Mighty never asked him to lunch any more, but Mr Binkle tried not to mind. He gave pennies to the children, and bones to hungry dogs, and saucers of milk to stray cats – and when next he saw the old dame he gave her back her boots and ten silver coins as well. She was surprised!

And now Mr Binkle is very happy, because the people of Fuff village like him, and make quite a fuss of him. But if ever he gets a little bit pleased with himself, he frowns and says: "Mr Binkle, be careful. Remember those boots!"

A Story of
Magic Strawberries

Once upon a time there lived a king called Framboise, who was very, very rich. He loved money. He was very greedy, very mean, and very cunning. His people were made to give him money for this and money for that, until they became very poor, and could afford nothing but the cheapest things to eat and the poorest things to wear.

They did not dare to grumble, for if they did the King told his soldiers to take them to prison, and off they went.

King Framboise was fat, for he loved food. He always dressed himself in the grandest clothes, for though he was mean, he was also vain. He loved to drive through the city in his gold carriage, drawn by twelve white horses, and see all his poor people bowing to him. Then he felt very grand indeed.

"I am a wonderful king," he thought. "No other king has as much money as I do, or can dress so finely."

Now, it happened one day that a stranger came to the country of King Framboise. He was an odd little fellow, dressed in brown and green, with the merriest twinkling eyes you could imagine. He played jolly tunes on a flute, and sounded just like a happy blackbird.

He walked happily up the village

street, whistling on his flute, and all the folk peeped out to see him.

"Come out and dance to my music!" he cried, and played a merry jig.

One by one the people came out, but they were so poorly clad, and so thin, that the flute player stared. "Why do you starve yourselves so?" he cried. "Surely your fields provide you with food to fatten your cheeks and put dancing into your feet."

"Our King takes most of our money," whispered a woman to him. "And what is left is barely enough to keep ourselves."

The flute player looked sad as he went to the next village. He stopped and looked at the tumbledown cottages.

"Hey, folk!" he cried. "Why don't you mend your houses?" And then he played such a merry tune that all the villagers came out to hear.

But he couldn't make them dance. It is only happy people who can dance, and they were some of the saddest people in the whole world.

"We don't have enough money to get

our houses mended," they told him. "The King takes so much from us, and we dare not refuse him."

The little man looked sadder still. He spent the night at the village, and heard much more before he set off on his journey again the next day.

Soon he arrived at the King's city. As he was walking through it, he heard a great trumpeting, and down the street came the King in his golden carriage, looking very splendid, very fat, and very rich.

The flute player stood and stared at him.

"You are vain," he thought, "and you

are fat and greedy. You are also rich! Now, how can I use these things for the good of your people?"

He went away and thought. Then a smile came over his face, and he chuckled.

He went to a strawberry field, and for two pieces of silver was allowed to pick the biggest strawberries he could see. They were very ripe and very red, and soon the flute player had an enormous basket full of the biggest strawberries that had ever been seen.

Then he put them down in a corner of the field and blew a magic tune over them. And all the time he smiled and smiled.

That afternoon he took the basket of strawberries to the street outside the palace, and walked up and down, crying, "Strawberries! Strawberries! Juicy and sweet, the finest in the world! Strawberries! Strawberries!"

The King happened to hear him shouting, and went to the window. He saw the basket of delicious strawberries, and his mouth watered. He was very fond of strawberries.

"Ask that fellow how much his strawberries are," commanded the King.

A footman ran down the street.

"Tell His Majesty that I paid two pieces of gold for them, and I want three, for I had to pick them in the hot sun," answered the flute player. The footman told the King.

"Much too dear, much too dear!" said His Majesty. "The fellow is nothing but a cheat. Go down and tell him I will give him one piece of gold, and even that is too much."

The footman went down and told the flute player.

"I'm sorry," he said, "but the strawberries are mine to sell at what price I choose. And three pieces of gold is the price."

When the King was told this answer, he grew angry. He meant to have the strawberries, but he didn't mean to pay anything like such a high price as three gold pieces for them.

"Tell the fellow to bring them up, and I will pay him," he said.

So the flute player brought his big basket of strawberries to the King. Footmen set them out on a great gold dish, and put them in front of King Framboise, who began to eat them at once.

You will hardly believe it, but he ate them all, every one!

When he had finished he held out just one single piece of silver to the flute player.

"Here," he said, "they are not worth three pieces of gold. They are not even worth one piece of gold. Take this silver piece and be gone."

"Your Majesty," said the flute player
sternly, "I want my three pieces of gold!"

The king frowned angrily.

"Soldiers, seize him and put him out!"
he cried.

But before the flute player could be
seized, he put his flute to his lips and
played a strange little tune. Then he
laughed, bowed, and ran from the palace.

King Framboise was just going to order
his soldiers to go after him, when he felt
something creaking inside his head.

He felt very funny. Something strange

was happening to his head. Could it be growing bigger? No, things like that don't happen suddenly, thought the King, puzzled and frightened.

Then he looked at his soldiers. They were all staring at him in the greatest surprise and astonishment. Then one by one they turned away from him to hide their smiles.

King Framboise got up and went across to the mirror. What he saw there made him stare with horror and amazement.

His head was shaped just like a big strawberry!

There were his little eyes, his big nose, and his mean mouth, just as usual – but, dear me, they seemed quite lost in his great strawberry-shaped head that sat on his collar as if it were ready to be picked.

"It's magic!" he gasped. "Those straw-berries were magic! Fetch that flute player, quick!"

The soldiers rushed out, laughing, and hunted for the flute player. They soon

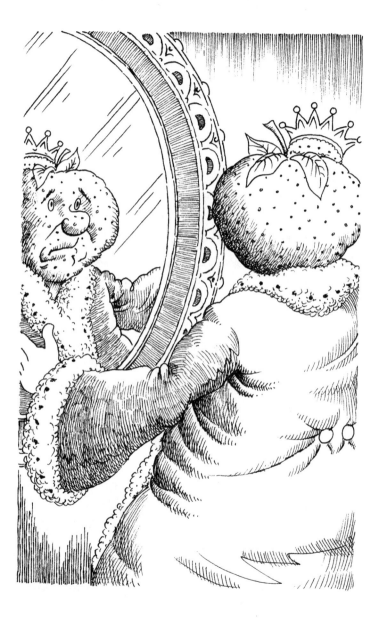

found him and brought him back, taking care to be very polite, in case he decided to use his magic on them, as well as on the King.

When the King saw him, he roared at him.

"Strawberry seller! What do you mean by this? Do you want to be put in prison for the rest of your life?"

"No," answered the little man, smiling. "Ha-ha! Excuse me laughing, but you do look funny! Your people will smile for once, when they see you now!"

"See me! I'll never let them see me like this!" shouted the King. "Use your

magic and make my head become its proper shape!"

"No, no," said the flute player. "It is a punishment for you!"

The King almost choked, he was so angry.

"Off with his head!" he cried to the soldiers. "Off with his head!"

"Remember," said the flute player, "whatever you do with my head will not alter yours! I am the only person who can take the spell away, and if you kill me, you will be strawberry-headed for the rest of your life. You will forever be known as King Strawberry Head!"

The King sat silent. It was true. This little flute player was the only one who could undo what he had done. He certainly musn't kill him!

"Leave me alone to speak with this man," said the King at last to his soldiers.

They went from the room. The King stared at the little man.

"Here are four gold pieces!" he said. "That is one more than you asked for. Take them and cure me quickly."

The little man laughed.

"I want more than that!" he said. "I want half the gold you have in your treasury."

The King was too astonished to speak. What did the fellow mean? Was he mad?

"No, I'm not mad!" said the flute player, reading the King's thoughts. "I want half the gold in your treasury!"

"But, goodness gracious, you don't suppose I'd give you that much, do you?" squealed the King in anger. "You would completely ruin me!"

"Stuff and nonsense!" answered the flute player. "You are the richest man in the world, and your people are the poorest folk on earth. You take their money to hoard for yourself, to buy your grand robes and to feed your great appetite. Your people live in hovels and eat little. They do not have any dancing in their feet, nor laughter in their eyes. I'd say you should be ashamed, King Framboise!"

The King grew red all over his great strawberry-shaped face.

"It is not true," he said.

"But I say it is," said the little man. "You big, rich, vain, greedy thing! How everyone will laugh at you!"

The King felt very sorry for himself. Whatever in the world was he to do? He hated the idea of giving so much away to this horrid little strawberry seller.

"Put on your coat, and wrap up your head in my scarf," said the flute player to King Framboise suddenly. "I want to take you outside and show you a few things."

"No, no," cried the King, "I won't go out like this!"

"You will!" said the little man – and the King did.

He was taken through the city. The

flute player showed him this and that, the thin children and the poorly dressed men and women, the sullen faces and the sad eyes. He heard how the people grumbled about him, and how much he was hated. Nobody knew that this big man with the odd-shaped head was the King.

King Framboise's ears began to burn and he wanted to go away and hide. How awful to be hated like that!

"I didn't know!" he whispered to the

flute player. "I didn't know! I didn't know!"

"No. You were too wrapped up in your selfishness to bother about anything else!" said the little man scornfully.

When they were back at the palace, the flute player looked at the King.

"Well," he said, "what about that money? Are you going to give it to me?"

"What would you do with it?" asked the King.

"Give it back to your people!" was the answer. "It rightfully belongs to them!"

The King sat for a long time without saying anything.

"I ought to do that, not you," he said at last. "If I took it from them, it is I who should give it back. I will treat my people better in the future, and perhaps I may win their love."

Suddenly he stopped speaking and put his hands to his head. Something was happening! Whatever was it?

"Is my head growing larger?" cried the King. "Oh dear! Oh dear! Oh dear!"

He rushed to the mirror and gazed

into it in astonishment. "Why!" he cried, "it's all right again! It's the same shape that it was this morning! The spell has been broken!"

"You broke it yourself!" said the flute player, smiling at him. "I wish you good evening. My work is done!"

And to the astonishment of the King he went gaily dancing from the room, playing on his flute the merriest tune ever heard, and vanished in the darkness outside.

King Framboise sat and felt his head

and thought. And the result of his deep thinking was that he took half of all his gold and gave it back to the people. More than that, he promised he would treat them well and rule them kindly, and he kept his word.

He wondered if his soldiers remembered his strawberry-shaped head, but when he asked them, they looked puzzled, and said no, they could remember nothing so strange as that.

Then the King wondered if he had had a dream, and offered a large reward to anyone who would bring him news of a little flute player, dressed in brown and green.

But no one ever did, and the flute player has never been heard of from that day to this. And, though nobody could think why, King Framboise never ate strawberries again – but I expect you could easily guess the reason, couldn't you?

Oh,
Mr Meddle!

Now, one day a strange thing happened to Mr Meddle. He went out into the town for a walk, and trotted round looking into one shop after another.

When he passed the butcher's shop a piece of paper blew out. It had been wrapped round a very juicy piece of meat. Mr Meddle didn't notice it, and he trod heavily on it. It stuck fast to the bottom of his shoe.

On went Mr Meddle, not knowing at all that he had a smelly, meaty bit of paper on his shoe. But, dear me, the very first dog he passed smelled that paper and came after him!

He padded at Mr Meddle's heels, sniffing hopefully. Mr Meddle turned and saw him. "Ah, nice dog, good dog, then!"

he said. "Trying to make friends with me, are you?" And he gave the surprised dog a pat on the head.

Pretty soon he passed another dog, and he also came sniffing up. He at once followed at Mr Meddle's heels, too, and Mr Meddle was rather surprised.

"I didn't know that dogs liked me so much," he said, and he patted the second dog as well. "Funny how animals like some people and not others. Well, it's nice to be liked."

On he went again and he hadn't gone very far before he collected yet another dog, rather a big one this time. He

bumped his nose quite hard into Mr Meddle's heels, and growled rather fiercely at the other two dogs.

"Now, now!" said Mr Meddle, stopping. "Good gracious me, here's another dog! What a peculiar thing that they should all take such a liking to me today."

He went on, feeling rather proud to have three dogs following him. Two more came up to see why the others were following Mr Meddle. That made five.

By this time people were beginning to feel surprised. Five dogs! Did they all belong to Mr Meddle?

"How well-trained your dogs are," said one man to Mr Meddle. "Following so well at heel like that!"

Mr Meddle felt pleased, though he wished the dogs wouldn't sniff round his feet so noisily whenever he stopped. The very big one trod on his toes, too.

Three more dogs joined the collection, and now Mr Meddle was being stared at by everyone he met. What a lot of dogs! They had never seen anyone taking so many for a walk before – and all trying to keep so close to his heels, too! Most remarkable.

Then the dogs began to growl at one another. The big dog snapped at a little one and nearly took a bite out of Mr Meddle's left heel. He stopped at once. "Now then! Behave yourselves, you dogs! I won't have any fighting!"

Well, Mr Meddle could say that a hundred times if he liked – the dogs weren't going to take any notice. One dog flew at another, and almost tripped Mr Meddle over. He felt rather alarmed.

"It's time you all went home now," he said firmly to them. "Go home! Good dogs, go home! I've taken you for a nice long walk, but now I'm tired of you. GO HOME!"

All the dogs were trying their hardest

to get at the bit of meaty paper underneath Mr Meddle's shoe. Mr Meddle thought they were trying to bite him, and he felt more alarmed than ever.

He began to walk away as fast as he could. The dogs followed at once. Mr Meddle ran. The dogs ran, too. Mr Meddle raced at top speed, and the dogs bounded along all round him, almost tripping him up.

He panted along, longing to reach his Aunt Jemima's house and get safely in at the front door. Bother these dogs! He didn't want to be liked by so many dogs.

They barked and bounded round him and people began to laugh. At last Mr Meddle saw his aunt's little house. He tore in at the front gate with all the dogs after him. His Aunt Jemima came to the front door to let him in – and good gracious me, not only Mr Meddle pushed in, but about a dozen frisky, excited dogs, too!

"MEDDLE!" said Aunt Jemima, in a really awful voice. "MEDDLE! What is the meaning of this? Take your dogs out."

"They won't leave me," wailed Mr Meddle. "I can't help it if dogs like me, Aunt Jemima."

"It's the first time they ever did," said his aunt. "Is this a joke, Meddle? One of your very silly jokes?"

"No, Aunt!" wailed Mr Meddle, trying to push away the dogs. His aunt got a newspaper and rolled it up.

"Now, you dogs," she said, "go home!" Then *whack, whack, whack*, went that newspaper, and Mr Meddle got some of the whacks as well as the dogs.

One of the dogs made a dash for Mr Meddle's shoe and tore off a bit of the meaty paper – and then Mr Meddle guessed why so many had followed him!

In a panic he took off his shoes and flung them out of the window.

Out went all the dogs after them, and Mr Meddle shut the window with a bang.

His aunt stared at him in amazement. "Meddle! What possessed you to throw your shoes out of the window? Have you gone mad? Look at those dogs tearing them to pieces."

"I never want to see a dog again," groaned poor Mr Meddle. "Never, never!"

"You go and chase them out of my front garden," said his aunt, grimly.

But Mr Meddle wouldn't go, so he got a bit more of the newspaper himself, and the dogs, having bitten the shoes to pieces, and each swallowed a small bit of the meaty paper, went off happily down the road.

"Now, Meddle," said his aunt. "You can go out into the garden and rake over the beds those dogs have run across. Then you can come back and scrub this floor and get rid of their dirty pawmarks."

"I don't want to," said Mr Meddle, who was feeling quite tired out.

But he had to. And now he is wondering what he is going to do about shoes, because his second pair are being mended at the cobblers, and we all know what happened to his first pair.

"You'll have to go out in your old bedroom slippers," said his aunt Jemima. "That will teach you to encourage all the dogs in the village to follow you, and then to bring them into my house. It will be cats next, I suppose!"

"It won't," said Mr Meddle, putting on his dreadful old bedroom slippers. "I'm not encouraging anything again – not even butterflies!"

Plum
Jam

"I wish I had some plums to make plum jam," said Lightfoot the pixie to Prickles. Prickles the hedgehog was her neighbour. He lived under the hedge where Lightfoot had her tiny house.

"Buy some," said Prickles.

"I haven't any money," said Lightfoot. She never had! She left her purse about everywhere, and the little red imps were always running off with it.

"Well – go and ask Mr Frowny for some," said Prickles. "Go on! Take your basket with you. He's got a lot of plum trees, and there are quite a lot of plums on the ground. He doesn't even bother to pick them up!"

"Oh, I daren't ask him," said Lightfoot. "He's always so cross, and he's got such

186

dreadful eyebrows to frown with. I wouldn't ask him for anything. You go, Pickles. Can't you go for me? If you will, I'll give you a pot of my plum jam all for yourself. You can spread it on the toadstools you like to eat so much and make a meal of toadstool and jam. Lovely!"

"It does sound nice," said Prickles. "Well, I'm not afraid of Mr Frowny. He can waggle his big eyebrows at me all he likes, and I shan't mind a bit!"

"All right, then – you go along," said Lightfoot. And Prickles ran off, his little bright eyes looking round and about for slugs as he went. He liked a meal of slugs. He thought they were even nicer than beetles.

He came to Mr Frowny's house. Mr Frowny was in his garden, weeding. Prickles ran up to him. "Please, Mr Frowny, may I have some of your plums?"

"What! Do you think you can climb trees and pick plums?" said Mr Frowny.

"Oh, no. But I could take some of those that are on the ground," said Prickles.

"And how many could you take in that little mouth of yours?" said Mr Frowny. "You need your legs to run with, so you can't carry any with those. Ho, ho! You could only take half a plum, Prickles!"

"Well, may I go and take some, Mr Frowny?" asked Prickles. "Please say yes. I'll do you a good turn, if you like, in payment."

"And pray what good turn can you do me?" asked Mr Frowny, waggling his enormous eyebrows to scare Prickles.

But Prickles wasn't a bit scared. "Please, sir, I will come and gobble up all your slugs," he said. "They feast on your lettuces, don't they? Well, I'll save your lettuces if I eat up all your slugs!"

"Very well," said Mr Frowny. "You can go and take as many plums as you can carry – but you'll only be able to carry half a plum in that silly mouth of yours. Ho, ho, ho!"

Prickles ran off. He went into the orchard, and he looked for a plum tree. Ah, there was one, a nice early tree, thick with little round red plums. Lovely!

Prickles ran to the tree. There were such a lot on the ground. Did he pick them up in his small mouth, or try to carry some off in his front paws?

No, he had a much better idea than that! What do you think he did? He curled himself tightly into a ball of prickles, and then he rolled himself round and round and round under the plum tree, among all the fallen plums.

What happened? Why, a great many plums stuck to his prickles! When he uncurled himself at last there were the plums, sticking all over him.

He ran out of the gate, and Mr Frowny saw him. He stared in surprise. "Hey! What's the matter with you? You do look odd! My goodness me – you're stuck all over with plums! So that's how you're going to take them away. Come back!"

But Prickles didn't come back. He scuttled down the lane, into the field, and ran down the hedge till he came to where Lightfoot was sewing outside her little house. She jumped up with a squeal.

"Oh! Whatever's this! Gracious – it's you, Prickles – but what have you done to yourself?"

"Brought you some plums to make plum jam, of course," said Prickles proudly. "Aren't I clever? Now you just take them all off my prickles one by one, Lightfoot, and wash them. Then get out your sugar, ready to make jam. You will be able to make a nice lot!"

"You clever little thing!" cried Lightfoot. "I'd kiss you if there was anywhere to kiss!"

"There's my nose," said Prickles. "But I don't much like being kissed. I'd rather have a pot of jam."

"You shall have one!" said Lightfoot, pleased. "I'll make you some straight away, and we'll have it for tea. You must come to tea with me today."

She set to work to make the jam. Soon

it was bubbling on the little stove, smelling very good indeed. Prickles sniffed hard. It would be very nice to spread on toadstools!

He went to tea with Lightfoot that afternoon. Outside her tiny house grew a little ring of toadstools. Prickles spread some plum jam on the top of one, and then nibbled it all round the edge till it was gone.

"Delicious!" he said. "Best I ever tasted. Thank you very much, Lightfoot."

"Now you take this pot away with you, and you can spread plum jam on your toadstools every day," said Lightfoot. "You deserve it for your cleverness!"

Prickles kept his word to Mr Frowny. He ate all his slugs for him, and now Mr Frowny has the finest lettuces in the town. So, you see, everybody was pleased!